M000073864

To Maurette,

Thank you

for your support.

God's blessing

to you.

Barb

BNewell572@aol.com

All I Ask

All I Ask

Barbara Keaton

INDIGO

Indigo is an imprint of
Genesis Press, Inc.
315 Third Avenue North
Columbus, Mississippi 39701

Copyright © 2000 by Barbara Keaton

All I Ask

All rights reserved. No part of this publication may be repro-
duced or transmitted in any form or by any means, electronic
or mechanical, including photocopy, recording, or any information storage and retrieval system, without permission in
writing from the publisher.

ISBN 1-58571-009-1

Set in Bookman Old Style

Manufactured in the United States of America

FIRST EDITION

I would like to thank God, my almighty creator and his Son, Jesus Christ, for the gift of the love of the written word. My mom, MY Girl, Aurelia Keaton, the woman who gave me life, love and strength! My brother, Shelvin and his family, my monsters, Stephanie and Matthew (and his wife Mattie—the only woman I know that can turn a nickel into a dollar!!) To my other babies, Kenny Jr. and Lauren, and my forever sister, Sharon. A special shout to Pam (Wynelle) & Yogie (Sylvia)—I gots nuttin but love for ya! And to Genesis Press—thanks for giving me a shot at my dream! Thanks to you all for being in my corner!

To Stephanie and Matthew
The loves of my life, the lights on my highway!
And to Mark
This world is made for dreamers—come dream
with me.

Chapter One

"Wear something hot," Shari admonished, but Deb felt she didn't own hot. To her, everything in her closet was practical, sensible, conservative. And the outfit she chose this night was exactly what she felt most comfortable in. Still Shari's words made her feel overly self-conscious about her choice.

Then to top it off, she had let Shari talk her into going to their soror's annual Labor Day card party. It wasn't that Deb didn't enjoy Denise's, but she was in no mood to socialize—especially not with any males. The phone call from her ex-boyfriend had left her drained and weary.

"I wish you had worn that little dress I asked you to," Shari whispered into Deb's ear as the pair stepped out of Shari's Mazda and strolled around the side of the house to the backyard.

"What's wrong with what I have on?" Deb raised her brows. The orange button-down shirt, white jeans, and matching orange shoes were quite appropriate for an outdoor party.

"Your outfits are boring." Shari paused to eye the large crowd in the backyard.

"Hey sorors." Denise ran to Deb and Shari. She hugged them tightly.

"Don't you think Deb's outfit is boring?" Shari asked Denise.

"Don't start, Shari. I'm not in the mood."

"Actually, Shari, I think the outfit is her." Denise stood back and surveyed Deb's attire. "Yup, it's you."

Deb ignored them both and walked farther into the yard. Shari and Denise joined her.

A chubby-faced woman waved. "Say, Shari and Deb, what's up?"

They waved back and glanced curiously at each other.

"Who is she?" Deb asked.

"I don't know. I thought you knew her?"

"I think she went to college with us. Hey, Denise, what's her name?"

"I don't know, but when y'all find out, let me know," Denise replied, then walked away.

Deb and Shari maneuvered through the crowd of familiar and unfamiliar faces. When Shari gravitated toward a group of men, Deb took that as her cue to step over to several groups of card tables set up for Bid Whist. She requested "next" at one of the tables and sat down on a nearby lawn chair. She rolled her eyes at Shari as she walked past. Moments later, Shari returned and handed Deb a cup of wine.

"Sip this," she ordered. "It'll make you blend in."

Deb sucked her teeth. She wanted to snatch the glass from her hands. Instead, she sipped the wine and looked over in time to see Shari give her a nod of approval. She turned her head to watch the crowd. Most of them mingled, but there were a few like her, camped out in a chair with a cup or bottle of beer plastered to their hands. She thought of Mario's call. The audacity of him. How could he be so cavalier. He acted as if nothing was wrong. She had asked him on more than one occasion to stop calling her. It seemed as if he called every month. Maybe he was checking up on her.

"Is this seat taken?" a deep voice asked.

"No." Deb answered. She didn't bother to look up.

"May I?" he asked. She could see his hand out of the corner of her eye as he pointed to the deep green chaise lounge to her left.

"Sure."

"My name is Darrin, what's yours?"

"Deborah." Her voice was flat. She was in no mood to be cordial. All she wanted to do was play a few hands of Bid Whist, socialize a little, and then leave. She stared into her cup.

"Am I disturbing you?" Darrin asked. "I can move if I am."

It was apparent this guy didn't know when he was being ignored. Probably was one of those spoiled children who couldn't take no for an answer.

"Let's try this one more time," he said, his voice stronger. "If I'm disturbing you, then I can take this chair and move."

She glanced at him. His eyes were on her face. She stared back. His eyes were a dark, mysterious black—the deepest, darkest set of eyes she had ever seen.

"Forgive me. I...I didn't mean to be rude."

He extended his right hand. She returned the gesture. His grip was firm, yet soft. She quickly pulled her hand from his.

"That's okay," he replied and smiled at her.

"Well, most people call me Deb. Did I hear you say your name's Darrin?"

"You were paying attention."

"I guess I was at that."

"Do you always treat strangers this way?"

"Only the ones who wears socks with their sandals." She regretted her comment the minute she said it. She waited for his reaction. His upper lip nearly touched the tip of his nose, as he looked down to his feet. He began to laugh heartily. Deb raised her eyebrows at the deep laughter. It seemed to come from his soul. It wasn't one of those polite laughs.

"My sister told me not to wear the damn things, but I hate to be cold." He crossed his legs and continued to laugh.

"I'm sorry for that. That was tacky."

"Not a problem. You know, that's twice you've been sorry. Are you always sorry for speaking your mind?"

She looked straight into his eyes. She noticed the glint in them. She liked his eyes. They danced when he spoke. She turned her head and focused on the people in the yard.

"Well, do you?" he repeated.

"Do I what?" Deb glanced at his feet.

"Always apologize for speaking your mind?"

She tilted her head. "No, actually I rarely, if ever apologize for speaking out. It's just that I thought that maybe my off remark may have been a little rude."

"Not at all." He tapped her on the arm. "Hey, if you can't laugh at yourself then you certainly can't laugh at life. You agree?"

"Well said." She raised her cup. "I agree."

"So, did you come here alone?" Darrin looked around the yard.

Finally it was out. Another guy was going to play that tired game of "guess who she's dating." Deb sighed.

"No, as a matter of fact I didn't."

"Oh, I see. Does he mind you talking to strangers?"

"As a matter of fact, the person I came with would love for me to talk to strangers."

She saw a curious expression cross his face. And she followed his eyes as they darted around the yard, up into the faces of the men scattered about.

"Oh, he does? Why is that?" he asked and faced her.

"Well, this person feels that I don't get out enough. You know, meet enough men. So for now, you're safe." Deb winked.

Darrin laughed. "For now?"

"Yeah, until they become tired of watching you talk to me and then the interrogation begins."

"I'm not afraid of any interrogations, but what kind of man would let a beautiful woman sit alone, talking to some strange man and not care?" He leaned close. She could smell the sweetness of a breath mint mixed with a bold scent of spicy cologne. Her senses reeled. She had smelled that scent before.

"Who said anything about the person being a man?" Deb asked. She huffed at the look of embarrassment on his face.

"You didn't say it wasn't," Darrin countered. "Besides..."

Deb interrupted. "Most men always assume that you have to go to a party escorted by a man. Why can't I just be here, by myself, sipping some wine and enjoying the crowd? What is it? Don't know too many women who can go places alone?"

"I didn't mean to..."

She put her hand up to his face. "If you wanted to know if I was here with someone all you had to do was ask. You didn't have to do the normal male Cro-Magnon thing, beating the bush trying to figure out if I'm available or not. All you had to do was ask me and I would have told you the truth." Deb rose from the chair.

Typical. Why did men have to be so typical?

She headed out of the yard, up the back stairs, into the kitchen. Suddenly it hit her. The cologne Darrin wore was one of Mario's favorites. Ugh, that horrid scent. He was wearing that cologne the night I caught him with that hoochie lookin' woman.

Deb became incensed. The scent of the cologne mixed with what she thought was an awful childish ploy added to her already foul attitude. She was in no mood to play games. Now or ever. She let the screen door slam behind her and cringed. She hated the sound of a door slamming.

Deb rested her body against the kitchen sink which looked out over the yard. She closed her eyes and breathed deeply. She exhaled slowly,

opened her eyes, then faced the window. From
where she stood she could see Darrin, his head
bent slightly. There was something about him,
though, and she felt it. She didn't think it was neg-
ative, that much she knew. To her own surprise,
Deb didn't get the idea that this man was up to
playing mind games. As a matter of fact, he gave
off an air of pure confidence.

She continued to study him and leaned her body
further over the sink. He looked up, toward the
window, and Deb stepped back quickly. Still, she
was able to keep him in view, even if he could no
longer see her. She was sure of it as she studied
his long, muscular legs stretched out before him.
One hand rested lazily upon his thigh, the other
gripped a bottle of beer. He had beautiful eyes, she
couldn't erase from her mind. And he'd seemed
unfazed by her curt responses. A surge of regret
flooded her.

Oh that was smart, Deb.

The loud slam of the screen door jarred her.

"Sorry," Shari interrupted. "You know I saw
that little exchange. What happened?" Deb saw
that suspicious look on Shari's face, her hands
placed firmly on her hips. "And Deb, please don't
tell me you're ready to leave. I just met a real cutie.
Girl, one minute I see you smiling, talking to that
gorgeous guy, and the next you're stalking away
and slamming doors! What's his name?"

"Nothing. No. And Cro-Magnon."

"What?" Shari blinked. "Oh forget it. Deb, you're impossible. Anyway, what're you doing in here?"

"I just came in to refill my glass."

"Right. Deb, you're lying." Shari pointed to Deb's glass on the counter. "Your glass is half full. So, what's wrong?"

"Nothing," Deb snapped. "I'll be out in a moment." She saw the worried look on Shari's face and lowered her voice. "Really, Shari. Nothing happened. Nothing's wrong. Now, go on back outside. I'll be out in a minute. Okay?"

"Okay." Shari walked to the door. "Are you sure you're all right?"

"Yes, I'm sure. Now go." Deb forced a smile.

Deb watched Shari sway across the yard, nod at Darrin, then proceed to stand in front of a tall, stockily built man. She tossed her head back as she laughed and casually touched his arm.

Deb wished that she could meet and mingle with men as easily as Shari did, but it just wasn't that way with her. To Deb, Shari was a lot like her mom, always saw the good in people—no one was ever completely bad. As long as she had known Shari, they had been roommates since college, she always admired that trait in her. But over the last two years Shari had become overly protective. Even more so after Deb's break up with Mario, then the death of her mom a month after. Deb appreciated Shari's concern, but she felt smothered by it. She felt more like a child to Shari than a best friend and soror.

The thought of her mother caused her to become solemn. Tears slowly streamed from her eyes. It had been months since Deb had felt this way, yet instead of fighting them she let the tears flow freely—allowed the thoughts to run wild.

She leaned heavily against the sink as images of her mother began to flood her. At first they were pleasant, only to be replaced with ones of her mother lying in a hospital bed, her body thin and gaunt from chemotherapy treatments, her face that of a brave warrior. On that day they held each other, Deb with her head in her mother's lap, her mother stroking her hair. And when her mother died two days later, Deb knew that a piece of her had died too.

"Forgive me, I didn't mean to interrupt," Darrin whispered as he let the door shut silently behind him.

"You didn't interrupt." She quickly wiped away the tears with the back of her hand. She refused to turn around. She didn't want him to see her tear-streaked face. Instead, she remained at the sink— the window allowed her to see his movements—and observed his large shoulders, his stealth-like motions as he opened the refrigerator door.

A sudden loud crash snapped Deb out of her trance as liquid gushed across the backs of her feet and shoes. She twirled to see Darrin amidst broken glass and beer foam, an apologetic look on his face. For the first time that evening Deb looked at him. Really looked at him.

His dark chocolate skin was baby smooth and his face was hairless with the exception of a thin, neatly trimmed mustache above his full lips. His perfectly round face was framed by a head full of dark curly hair, cut close. He stood at least six-foot-four, with a massive chest and large, muscular arms. His hands matched the smoothness of his skin, and his nails were trimmed and clean. But it was his eyes that drew Deb to him and she couldn't look away. His eyes were so mysteriously dark, an endless black that was intense, frighteningly intense.

"I am so sorry," Darrin began, his eyes frantically searched around the kitchen.

"It's okay." Deb grabbed a towel from the sink. "Denise won't shoot you, she'll just maul you for ruining her new floor."

Darrin looked dumbfounded as Deb handed him the towel. She headed to the pantry for the mop. She heard him curse just as she returned to the kitchen. He was bent over, holding his hand. It was bleeding.

"How did you do that?" Deb asked softly.

Darrin sighed. "I cut it picking up the glass.
That's why I like cans."

"Here, let me see that," Deb said and propped
the mop up against the refrigerator. She took him
by the hand. He stood, his eyes on her, and Deb
found herself locked by the darkness of his gaze.
She blinked a couple of times in an attempt to
break the strange hypnotic spell. He never moved
and she watched him watch her, his lips forming a
slight smile. The more he stared, the more Deb felt
as if he was trying to see into her, figure her out.
She forced herself to pay attention to his bleeding
hand.

"The bleeding's getting worse," Deb said and
grabbed several paper napkins. She wrapped them
around Darrin's hand and applied pressure.
"Darrin, we need to take this to the bathroom.
Denise keeps some gauze and antiseptic in there,
and it looks as if you need it."

"Will it hurt?" he asked, his voice was soft,
almost child-like.

"No, and if it does I will blow on it."

Darrin chuckled. "My mom used to do that."

"So did mine."

They made their way down the long corridor, she
led, his free hand in hers. She closed the door
behind them and motioned for him to sit on the
seat of the commode. Deb pulled out the first-aid
kit from under the sink and set it on top. She took

his hand in hers and looked over the cut. He sat, wide-eyed, as she removed a pair of scissors.

"What are you going to do with those?" He yanked his hand from hers.

"Cut the gauze, see?" She held up a roll of gauze.

"Oh," he replied.

She then retrieved some tape and antiseptic cream from the kit.

"Hold out your hand," Deb ordered.

"Are you sure this won't hurt?"

Deb rolled her eyes upward. "I said I would take care of you, didn't I?" She looked at the wound, pulled his hand over to the sink, and turned on the water. Darrin pulled his hand back again.

"You know if you use soap, it's going to really sting," he warned.

"I told you I would blow on it." Deb let out a long sigh. "I need to rinse this cut to make sure there isn't any glass in the wound."

"Deb, I really don't think there's any glass in it."

"Now, you don't know that." She chuckled. "You're a little too big to be such a baby."

"I don't like pain of any kind."

She ignored his comment. Surely there was a hidden meaning behind those words. She forceful-ly placed his hand under the warm running water. Darrin flinched as she gently applied soap, then let the water cascade over the wound.

"I like that, Deb. It feels better already." He gazed at her. Again, she got that feeling. He was searching for something. She tried to read him, tried to read the intensity. He sat close. She could feel his warm breath on the side of her face.

She told him to sit back as she applied the ointment followed by gauze. "Is that too tight?" she asked as she applied the tape.

He shook his head. "Uhmmm."

"Did I hurt you?"

"No, I was just thinking... Never mind."

She finished securing the gauze with white tape. "All done. You'll survive now." She stepped back and Darrin stood, but he didn't move away, he moved closer to her. The area around the back of her neck became warm when she witnessed that same glint in his dark eyes as he had when they stood in the kitchen.

Deb felt flustered. "Are...are you okay?"

"Yes, I'm fine."

"See, now did that hurt?"

"Actually, no, it didn't. You're a good nurse. Has anyone ever told you that?"

She was taken aback when he flashed her the most beautiful set of white teeth. Deb had seen smiles like his before. Killer smiles, she called them. The kind intended to get your attention, put you off your guard, and then tear you apart. It was the same kind of smile Mario would use to disarm her. She became tense, her body stiffening.

He backed away. "Thank you, Deb, for tending to my wound. But now I need to go back to the kitchen and finish cleaning up my mess."

"No problem. Any time. When I'm finished in here I will come and help you clean up."

"No, let me do it. You've helped me enough. Thank you, Deb," Darrin repeated. He stood over her for a long moment, scanning her from head to toe. She tried to stare back, to indulge in this game of wills. Deb wanted to see if she could match his intensity. A warm sensation moved across her shoulders and down her hands. She became oddly comfortable, almost safe. For a brief moment she felt as if she knew him, as if she had always known him. But she knew better. She had never laid eyes on him before tonight.

Now she was confused. She couldn't understand how she could have any feelings for someone she had just met. Someone she didn't even know. Her composure began to waver. He moved closer. She felt as if she was about to fall—no float—as his male scent assaulted her senses. His lips seemed to move in slow motion, but she didn't hear him speak. She was entrapped by the closeness of his body.

"Is anyone in there?!" a female voice called from the other side of the door.

Deb jumped. "Just a minute," she yelled out.

"Deb, thanks again," Darrin whispered as he released her hand and opened the door.

The woman looked from Deb to Darrin and back again with a quizzing look that slowly turned into a wicked grin. "Seems as if this is the place to be," she said in a low, seductive voice.

"I was just giving a little first aid, that's all," Deb countered.

"Sure, honey. Whatever you want to call it is fine by me," the woman replied and dismissed Deb with a nonchalant wave of her hand. She never took her eyes off Darrin. And in one fluid motion she moved around Deb, pushed her slightly to one side, and slid closer to Darrin, her breasts inches from his body.

"Give me a chance to clean up this mess and the room is all yours," Deb said sharply.

"Whatever." The woman stayed right by Darrin's side. Deb felt the hot anger rise up her neck. She was sure her caramel colored face was a blazing red—her jaw taut.

"Excuse me," Darrin said politely, carefully stepping around the woman and out of the bathroom.

"Sorry, honey, I'm not trying to step on nobody's toes. He's all yours if you want him."

"I don't even know him," Deb shot back.

"Whatever. Are you almost finished? I gotta go real bad." The woman placed her hands on her hips as she poked her head out of the bathroom and watched Darrin walk away.

Deb cleaned up the bathroom and left. The woman slammed the door behind her. Deb was perplexed. She couldn't understand why she had reacted the way she did over a man she hardly knew. She wasn't the least bit interested in Darrin. Not the least bit.

Denise and Shari stood in the kitchen door. Both had mischievous grins on their faces. "What were you two doing in the bathroom?" Denise asked.

"You guys are horrible." Deb pushed past them into the kitchen.

The shadows let her watch Darrin, bent over, his back to her, as he cleaned up the broken glass. His body moved gracefully, his broad shoulders flexing as he carefully picked up the remaining pieces of broken glass.

"What'd you spill, Darrin?" Denise asked behind Deb's back.

Deb jumped at the sound of her soror's voice and turned to see both Denise and Shari behind her. The pair exchanged sideways glances then looked at Deb, their eyebrows raised. Darrin lifted his head. She was caught. Deb walked quickly into the kitchen, grabbed a towel and began to assist Darrin in cleaning up the spill. She wanted to avoid her two sorors.

"Denise, you know me. I love to make a mess. I dropped a bottle of beer, tried to clean it up, and cut myself. Deb was nice enough to administer first aid." Darrin held up his bandaged hand.

"Well, you're in good hands with Deb." Denise elbowed Shari.

"Yeah, she's real handy." Shari said.

Deb clinched her teeth. "Don't you have guests to attend to? And Shari, don't you have something to chase?"

"Well, playtime is over. We'll see you two outside." Denise pulled Shari by the arm and headed out into the yard.

"Here, let me get that." Deb pushed Darrin's hand. "I don't want you to cut yourself again."

"No, I don't want that, but if I do will you promise to fix me up again, Nurse Deb?" Darrin touched Deb's hand. She quickly pulled her hand away.

As they cleaned they stole silent glances at each other. She looked toward the screen door. Shari and Denise peered at them and whispered.

"Okay, Frick and Frack," Deb called toward them.

"What?" Denise said, an amused look on her face. "We aren't doing anything, are we, Shari?"

"Not a thing," Shari agreed.

Darrin saw the two standing there. Shari and Denise quickly replaced their devilish grins with

angelic smiles. Darrin looked at Deb, smiled warmly, and joined her at the kitchen sink.

"How long have you known Denise?" Darrin
asked and turned on the water.

"She and I are sorors."

"You guys went to college together?" Darrin
removed the towel from Deb's hand and rinsed it
out.

"Yeah, as well as Shari. We all used to live
together." Deb shifted her body. She wanted to
avoid the warmth of his body next to hers. "Well,
all's finished here. I'm going to go outside and try to
play a hand or two of bid. I'll see you later." She
waved and headed for the door.

Darrin stopped her, tapping her lightly on the
arm. He stammered, then blurted out, "Thanks
again."

She nodded and continued out the door just in
time to sit down at a card table. He had not followed her, but she still felt his presence as she
shuffled the cards several times before handing
them over to her right for the cut. She dealt the
cards to the other players and settled back in the
chair.

Out of the corner of her eye she spied Darrin as
he walked slowly down the steps. He paused, then
moved to a lawn chair located a few feet away from
her. When he sat down, Deb noticed how he casually folded his large over his chest as he stretched

out his long, muscular legs, one crossed over the other. She laughed to herself.

The socks were gone.

Chapter Two

Deb forced herself to focus on the card game, trying to read her partner, one of Denise's unknown
guests, who had the most evil pair of eyes she had
ever seen on a man. Through several hands and
three new sets of players, her partner glared at her.
After about an hour, the two lost on a no-trump.
Deb shook her partner's hand, got up from the
table, and headed back to the kitchen.

It was only when she heard the screen door slam
shut that she realized the man had followed her.
He stood there leering at her.

"Would you like a beer?" Deb asked and opened
the refrigerator.

"Yeah." He breathed noisily. "You know that
was some bad ass card playing, girl. Where you
learn to play like that?"

"My brother taught me," she answered curtly.

"You play well, you know that? We should get
together sometime. To play cards of course." He
grinned.

"No. I don't play that often."

He moved closer. "We really should get together."

Deb stepped away from the refrigerator until her
back was squarely up against the wall. "I don't

think so. I work a lot, so I don't get out much." She
tried to sound indifferent. She also tried to move
around the intruder, but each time she did, he
moved with her. As he drew even closer, she could
smell the liquor on his breath.

"But you and I would have so much fun," he
mumbled.

He stared so long that Deb began to feel as if he
could see right through her. She shifted her body
slightly to the right, and again he moved with her,
this time placing his hands above her head against
the wall. His face came closer as he leaned down
and tried to kiss her. She tried to shove him away.

"Why you want to be like that?" he asked. "We
could really be good together and you know it!"

"Brother, I don't think so," Darrin said tersely
from the doorway.

"Oh? She's already agreed to go out with me.
Haven't you?" he responded. He turned slightly to
study Darrin, then slid closer to Deb again.

"No, I don't think she did." Darrin stepped forward. "As a matter of fact, she's going out with
me." His deep voice was harsh and angry.

Deb became frightened at the cold darkness she
saw in his eyes. They were mere slits as Darrin
walked toward them. His jaws were tight and the
vein in his neck pulsated.

"Deb, my dear, come over here," Darrin said. He
pulled her by the arm and stood between her and

her card partner. "Now, what was it that you wanted with her?" he said to the man as he towered over him. He stood at least five inches taller and was a solid fifty pounds heavier.

"Naw, chief, my fault, my fault." Deb's card partner tried to move, but Darrin blocked his way.

"You didn't answer my question."

"Yo, man. I don't mean no harm. Besides, I didn't see you, or anyone, talking to her, so I figured she was fair game."

"Well, she isn't," Darrin answered matter-of-factly. "So, how about you go on back outside. I think I heard someone call for a card partner."

"She's my partner."

"No, she isn't!" Darrin barked and poked him in his chest. "She was your partner. She's finished playing for the night." He faced Deb. "Deb, you are finished playing cards for the evening, aren't you?"

"Yo, man, ain't no thing. I'm finished for the night," Deb's card partner responded quickly. He placed his hands up over his head and moved timidly around Darrin. When he reached the door, he began to run. He stumbled out, missed the first two steps, and tumbled out onto the grass.

Snickers came from the crowd in the yard as the man got up, brushed himself off, and walked over to the card tables.

Deb looked at Darrin. The anger in his eyes was
gone. She was relieved. She didn't like what she
had seen in those dark eyes. It was too fierce.

"Would you like to sit on the porch?" Darrin
asked.

"No, I think I'm ready to go home."

"Are you sure?" he asked. "It's a really nice night
and there's a full moon."

"I'm sure. I'm tired and I have a project to work
on for my job."

"What kind of work do you do?"

"I'm a writer," she answered flatly. She knew he
was stalling. And she wasn't going to allow it.
True, she was grateful for the rescue from that
creep, but she wasn't about to get caught up with
him. Not tonight or any other night.

"Oh? Who do you write for?" he asked.

"I write for *Neighborhood Magazine*," she
responded. "But I really have to go." She walked to
the door.

"Maybe I'll see you again?" Darrin quizzed, eyebrows raised.

"Maybe," Deb answered. She stood at the top of
the porch and scanned the crowd for Shari. She
knew that Darrin was inches from her, only the
screen door separating them. She began to get that
feeling, the same one she had when she first sat
down to play cards. It was that look of his, those
dark intense eyes which bore through her. Deb's

body warmed again. She spotted Shari in a conversation with a medium built brown-skinned fel-
low. Deb stepped off the stairs and moved quickly
in Shari's direction. She realized she was almost
running and slowed down. She saw her former
card partner move swiftly in the opposite direction.
Deb laughed, looked back at the screen door.
Darrin stood in the doorway.

"Shari, I'm ready to go home."

"I'm not," Shari whined.

"Well, I'm leaving without you."

"Here." Shari shoved her car keys into Deb's
hand. "You're a trip."

"Now, what?"

"We'll talk about it later, but you go on home
now, you hear."

Deb gave her a curt goodbye and headed out the
yard. She stopped long enough to give cursory
farewells to a few people she knew. She saw Darrin
still at the door and switched course, heading for
the side exit. She wasn't interested in him—she
wasn't up to playing the "dating game" and trying
to get close, only to find out he was just like Mario,
a lying cheat. She reached Shari's car, put the key
into the ignition and shifted the gear into first. A
tall figure appeared in the rear-view mirror as she
pulled away from the curb.

He was friendly, Deb scolded herself. There was
no reason for you to run like that. Girl, I swear.

In the distance she could still see the figure getting smaller and smaller as she drove down Denise's street.

Deb sighed. I've got to protect myself. I can't get caught up into another no-win situation. I mean, I can't get hurt again. I've been there before and I will never let that happen again.

❂ ❂ ❂

Darrin walked back to the yard. He needed to talk to Denise before the night was over. He wanted to know all about Deb. But most of all he wanted to know who had put that pain in her eyes. Yeah, he had had his share of women, some he liked, one he loved, but he had never met a woman who made him react the way she did. He had never stepped up into another man's face the way he had stepped up to Deb's card partner Maybe he was losing it. All aside, he knew he didn't—wasn't going to give up.

"Darrin?" Denise stepped out onto the front porch. "Where's Deb?"

"She left." Darrin sat down on the front porch. "Said something about having an assignment due."

"Figures."

"Figures? What do you mean?"

"I mean, she's really busy. You know she's a writer for *Neighborhood Magazine*. Did she tell you that?"

"That's about all she told me. What's up with her, Denise?"

Darrin watched Denise. He knew it was off limits to test their friendship, their sisterhood, by asking personal questions. But he didn't want to leave without some hint that he might have a chance with Deb.

"Well, Darrin." She sat next to him. "I've known you a long time. But she's my sister. My soror. The only thing I can tell you is that she is available and..." Denise paused.

"And what?"

"And she's been hurt."

Darrin scanned the street. He rubbed his smooth face. He had to see her again. Some way, he felt he had to know her. How was a different story.

◎ ◎ ◎

Deb conversed with herself over and over as she weaved in and out of the late-night traffic, toward home. A car pulled up alongside. Two couples sat in the car. They pointed and laughed at Deb as she talked to herself. She stopped. The last thing she wanted was to be deemed insane. She glanced over

at the couples.   They were young, probably
teenagers. In the back sat a girl and boy. They sat
close, the boy stroking her long dark hair, his other
hand wrapped protectively about her shoulder.
There was a time when she and Mario sat like that
in a car.

Why am I thinking about that?

Deb continued to watch the romantic exchange.
She envied them—the open display of affection.
Their exchange reminded her of her own unhappi-
ness, the empty void that filled her days and
nights.

Behind her car horns blared. The traffic light
had turned green and Deb hadn't even noticed.
She waved into the rear-view mirror at the car
behind her, slammed her foot on the accelerator.
The tires screeched as she shot away from the light
and out into the intersection.

When she pulled into the driveway, she sat for a
moment. She knew her actions had been less than
stellar toward Darrin. Yet, her curt and short
behavior aside, he had still been kind to her. In his
eyes she thought she had seen a longing of sorts.
Or was it loneliness? It couldn't be the same loneliness she felt; he was far too handsome to be without a girlfriend. There had to be someone.

Rocket's loud bark snapped Deb out of her
thoughts. She climbed slowly out of the car, headed to the porch, and opened the door.

"Hey there, honey." Deb scratched behind the dog's ears. The dog's tail wagged wildly as she followed her to the stairs which led to her bedroom. Deb bent and faced Rocket. "You know you can't come upstairs tonight. Shari just cleaned the carpet and she'll kill both of us."

Rocket sat down and whined loudly.

Deb smiled at the pitiful look on the dog's face. "All right, you can come upstairs, but you have to stay in my room."

As if the dog fully understood her every word, she brushed past her, bounded up the stairs, and went directly into Deb's room. Deb shook her head as she climbed the stairway.

The phone rang, and Rocket barked wildly at the sound, a habit whenever the phone or the door bell rang. Deb had often told Shari that Rocket would make a good dog for the hearing impaired.

"Rocket, get off the bed," Deb admonished as she picked up the phone. "Hello?"

"Deb, this is Denise."

"No joke. Like after six years I wouldn't know it was you. Besides, who else other than you and Shari calls me after midnight?"

"Okay, smarty pants. What are you doing?"

She let out a long exasperated sigh. "Now, Denise, I know you didn't call me to ask that stupid camp question. So just spit it out." Deb wasn't in the mood for Denise's interrogations. Anger began to rise, but she settled into the mountain of pillows on her bed and braced herself for Denise's cross-examination and million and one questions.

"Girl, you are one mean cookie, you know that?"

"Yeah, yeah...get to the point, Denise."

Denise began her verbal dissertation about what folks were wearing, how it looked, who was dating whom and how Miss Thang shouldn't have cut her hair. Deb wasn't paying any attention. Her thoughts focused on Darrin as he stood in Denise's kitchen, dressed in tan linen pants and a matching short-sleeved shirt, his dark arms straining the fabric of his sleeves.

"Did you hear me?" Denise asked impatiently.

Deb mumbled something as her mind wandered back to Darrin and his dark eyes, his large hands in her small ones, his full lips close to hers, his breath warm and sweet.

"Deb?" Denise asked. "Are you paying atten- tion?"

"I'm sorry, Denise. What did you say?"

"Never mind. Anyway, Darrin asked about you."

She was surprised, the area around her neck flushing with anger—or was it something else? "Oh, really," she asked, trying to sound uninterest- ed. "What did he want? My number?"

"No, he didn't ask me for it. He just asked about you. Like what you do. How long I have known you.

If you are dating anyone in particular. You know, that kind of stuff."

Deb was disappointed. "And he didn't ask for my number?"

"If he had, and I gave it to him, you would have cussed me out and hung up on him."

"How do you know that?"

"Deb, sistergirl, I know you," Denise said.

As Deb had predicted, Denise went on and on for over twenty minutes about how happiness would forever elude her, what a good catch Darrin Wilson would be, and how Deb should give him a chance. "Deb, he's really interested in you." She finally said. "We talked for nearly an hour about you. You know he owns his own business?"

"And what's that supposed to mean to me?" Deb responded louder than she meant to. Rocket whined and moved from her favorite spot near the top of the bed to the floor. "Look, Ne, I'm tired." Deb sighed. "I've got to get up early and work on some research for a story, which is due first thing Monday morning, so I'll talk to you later."

"Wait, Deb, don't hang up. Are we still going to brunch tomorrow?"

"Oh, Ne, I'm sorry, I forgot. Yeah, we may go. It all depends on how much of this research I get finished."

"C'mon Deb, work hard. I've been looking forward to going to The Retreat for a long time. Besides, you promised."

"Okay, okay. I'll be there. But you better be at the restaurant at eleven o'clock or I will eat without you."

"Can I bring a friend?"

"I thought Shari was going."

"No, she said she meant to tell you she won't be going."

"Oh?"

"Yeah, she said something about having to see a man about a dog."

"Then, who is it Denise? It better not be Darrin," Deb responded. She tried to make the comment sound indifferent. But she silently hoped that Denise had invited Darrin.

"Dang Deb. You're really mean. You know that? I don't like who you've become since you broke up with Mario. Not all men are dogs."

"Umm, let you tell it."

"Anyway, it's not Darrin. It's the new guy, Jon."

"Oh, sure, bring him along. The more the merrier," Deb said sarcastically.

"Whatever, Deb. I'll see you tomorrow."

"Eleven sharp."

"Yeah, eleven o'clock, sharp. Oh, and Deb?"

"Yes, Denise."

"You need to let it go."

"Denise, I'm not in the mood, okay?" Deb snapped.

"I had to say it. Good night, soror. I love you."

Deb's mood softened. She was sorry for being so curt with her. "I love you too, Denise."

"Wait! Don't hang up! I almost forgot. Shari told me to tell you that she is spending the night here. She and Bruce are in a deep conversation and she 'just can't pull herself away,'" Denise said, imitating Shari's voice. "As a matter of fact, I can see her and Bruce laughing in each other's face. Nite-Nite, Deb."

"Goodnight, Denise." Deb hung up the telephone and looked at Rocket now spread out across the bed. "Why couldn't my life be simple?" she asked.

Deb dressed for bed. As she slipped into her silk chemise nightgown, she continued to think about Darrin and wished that someone would love and protect her, much like Rocket did, unconditionally.

Chapter Three

The line at the newly opened restaurant snaked around the corner and down the side of the building. Just opened two weeks prior, The Retreat was packed to capacity. Throngs of people waited, everyone dressed in their Sunday best.

The Retreat had become popular and was once the home of the Pullman Car Company's first general superintendent, Henry H. Sessions. Built in 1881, the home boasted several large wood-paneled rooms, and a wide cherry wood staircase. When Sessions left the Pullman Company, George M. Pullman, the owner of Pullman Rail Cars, turned the home into the Pullman Executive Club, which remained open until the 1950's. In 1992, Chef John Mayer bought the restaurant, and began catering to a clientele who enjoyed Cajun cuisine.

The three-story house was decorated in deep oak, with an oriental rug at the reception area. The expansive dining room was packed with large tables, each adorned in starched white table cloths and small floral arrangements.

Deb smiled politely as she moved past a small crowd of women standing near the door as she headed to the greeter. After she gave her name, she stood near a wall and watched the small group, listening as they chatted.

"And when they finish, that neighborhood will be like new," said a diminutive woman dressed in a blue sequined dress, a rhinestone choker at her neck, and black sequined shoes. Her bleached blonde hair was swept up neatly into a French Roll, held firmly in place with a rhinestone hair comb, ringlet curls cascading down the sides of her face.

Deb thought sequins at eleven o'clock in the morning was a bit ostentatious, then she looked down at her own outfit. She smoothed her hands across the front of her beige sleeveless, ankle-length sun dress. The small taupe and barely-blue flowers brought out the warmth of her complexion. She poked her right foot out slightly and took in the view of her fuchsia-painted toenails, brazen against the deep brown of her high-heeled, open-toed sandals. Shari had talked Deb into buying the sandals, saying that the shoes made her legs look even more shapely than they were.

As Deb waited, she switched between observing the sea of faces and the restaurant's menu. She had her head buried in the menu when she heard a familiar voice.

"Hi. I have a reservation for two. Wilson," the voice said.

She looked up from the menu. Darrin stood at
the reservation desk. That familiar chill returned
to run down her arms. He turned and spotted her.

"Well, I didn't think we'd see each other so
soon," Darrin said softly, his black eyes dancing.

"Yeah, nice to see you again," Deb answered flatly.

He gave her a strange look, stepped to her left.
His hand brushed lightly against her bare arm,
causing her senses to go into a tailspin.

"I have reservations for two. Wilson," Darrin
repeated to the hostess on duty. He flashed a wide
smile.

The young woman turned a deep shade of red
and her face took on a dreamy appearance. "Yes,
Mr. Wilson, your table is waiting. Right this way."

A tall beautiful woman stepped up and took
Darrin by the arm. Dressed in an impeccable
cream-colored crepe suit, with a pale peach blouse,
the woman's long curly hair rested lazily on her
shoulders, curls framing her round face. Her
smooth skin was the color of warm chocolate, and
her narrow nose jutted out from her face. She
smiled broadly and nodded her head slightly as she
acknowledged Deb. Deb noticed that the woman
was just a few inches shorter than Darrin, even
though she wore three inch, leather sling-back
pumps.

"Hump," Deb mumbled under her breath.

Darrin stopped. "It was nice seeing you again. I hope we get a chance to run into each other again—soon."

Deb's mouth was open. She was sure that steam was rising from around her collar. She became angry. No, jealous. She was jealous. How dare he ask Denise all those questions about her, then whisk in here with some woman on his arm.

Umph, yeah, nice to see you too. Men!

"Deb, you been waiting long?" Denise said, as she walked up behind Deb.

Caught off guard, Deb twirled around quickly. "What?" she said curtly.

"Woooa!" Denise took a step back. "Who pulled your chain and made you bark?"

"Nobody," Deb growled.

"Somebody had to. You got that 'I-ain't-playin' look on your face."

Deb dismissed Denise with a wave of her hand. "Never mind all that. I almost left. You're late."

"Geez, no 'How you doin'?' or 'Kiss my foot.' Well, it's nice to see you too, Deb, how are you? Besides, I'm only fifteen minutes late."

Deb inhaled deeply. She felt silly. She grabbed Denise and gave her a hug, and over her shoulder, Deb noticed a handsome guy standing behind them. They studied each other. Deb detected a hint of uncertainty in him.

"This is who I was telling you about." Denise beamed. "Jon Claude, meet Deb. Deb, meet Jon Claude."

Jon took a hesitant step forward.

"Don't worry, I'm not biting today," Deb joked and held out her hand. "Besides, I had my rabies shots last week."

"So nice to meet you. I've heard so much about you, I feel as if I know you." Jon pulled Deb into a tight, rib-crushing bear hug.

"Oh? What did she tell you about me?" Deb raised an eyebrow at Denise.

"Only good things. She told me you are a writer for *Neighborhood Magazine*."

"Yeah. And if I know Denise, that wasn't all. What else?"

"She also told me you are single and looking. You know I have a really good friend who's looking for a great woman. I think you two would hit it off. He's a salesman. Really nice. Just like you."

Deb flashed Denise a mean look. Denise elbowed Jon in his side. He gasped and gave her a "what'd I do?" look. Deb was undone. She couldn't believe that Denise was now advertising her as "lonely and looking." True, she hadn't wanted any parts of men. She had immersed herself in her work. But still, this wasn't fair of Denise. Deb shook her head and made a mental note to have a stern talk with her later.

"It's okay, Jon," she lied. It wasn't okay at all. "I know you mean well, but I'm not interested in meeting your friend."

The hostess stepped up to Deb. "Ms. Anderson, your table is ready, please follow me." She maneuvered smoothly around the closely situated tables and chairs, her hips swaying exaggeratedly from side to side, as she led the trio toward the rear, to a group of tables meant for four or less. Deb walked behind Denise and Jon, still smarting from Jon's comment. As she approached her seat, she saw Darrin and the young woman to her right. They were laughing and touching hands. Her jaw tightened as she watched the interaction. When Darrin smiled and looked directly at her, she quickly turned her head.

"Typical," she said.

Denise frowned. "What did you say?"

"Nothing. I'm starved. I believe I know what I want to order," Deb answered as she sat down across from Denise and Jon.

Deb took the menu from the hostess and held it high to hide her face. She didn't want to see Darrin and his woman. But as curiosity would gain the upper hand, Deb couldn't resist. She peered over the menu—his good looks and his dark eyes filled the room.

Denise chatted endlessly. She noticed that Deb was not paying attention and turned to see what had caught Deb's attention.

"Deb, I swear, I didn't know he would be here. Besides, that's his—"

"Denise, I'm not interested. Let's look over the menu so we can order, please."

Deb set the menu on the table. She looked up. Darrin was watching her, a curious look on his face. She refused to acknowledge the expression.

I don't even like him.

"Deb, did you hear that? Jon got a promotion," Denise said excitedly.

Deb nodded her head.

Denise and Jon sat there, their hands entwined, and told Deb how they met. Deb knew Denise had uncanny ways when it came to men. She seemed to meet them in the strangest situation, in some of the strangest ways. It was Denise who always insisted that the grocery store was a great place to meet men. Deb forced her attention to Denise as she repeated the story—for the umpteenth time—of how she and Jon met.

Denise made exaggerated movements with her hands as she described how she hit Jon with her cart, which in turn caused Jon to ram his cart into a display of canned vegetables.

"And of course cans were rolling all over the aisle!" Denise laughed. "We ended up chasing the cans and bumping into each other. The people in the store thought we were nuts, we were laughing so hard."

"Talk about glad to bump into you," Jon ended the story.

Denise continued to rattle on. And though Deb had laughed at the story, she couldn't shake the agitated state she was in. And she didn't want to have to sit and watch Darrin and another woman throughout their whole meal.

"I don't need any more time. I know what I want," Deb responded to the waitress, her tone short and snappy.

"Yeah, I also know what you need," Denise replied. She glowered at Deb.

Deb glanced over at Darrin for what she swore would be her last time. She forced herself to give all of her attention her to Denise and her new beau. Settling back in her chair, she listened intently to Denise and Jon and admired the ease of their interaction. Deb felt they made a perfect couple.

For once, Deb was relieved that Denise dominated the conversation. For over an hour she told stories, jokes, and talked about Jon, which gave Deb a chance to mull over something other than Darrin.

When the trio finished their meal, Deb noticed that Darrin's seat was already empty. Denise became silent as the they exited the restaurant and

walked toward their respective cars. Deb could see
that Denise was searching for something to say.

"It was nice meeting you, Jon." Deb shook his
hand.

He stood next to Denise, and Deb could have
sworn his expression was one of pity. This only
added to her already sour mood.

That's just great. Just what I need, a pity party.

She looked at Denise. "I'll talk to you later."

"I just know you will. See ya," Denise responded.

Deb turned quickly to leave. She cursed as she
walked. How could Denise tell him all about her
love life, or lack thereof? She promised not to let
Denise off the hook for this one.

She knew that Denise and Jon were still at the
corner where she left them, but she refused to turn
and continued to walk toward her Pathfinder. The
warm August day began to soothe her. She took in
the beauty of lush green lawns and tall oaks which
lined the block. It was days like this when the
memories of Mario stung the most. All the days
they spent together. The walks on the beach while
the sun rose, the days they spent making love.

How could she miss Mario? Was it because she
was really lonely? Why was she still thinking of
him? Deb quizzed as she fumbled with her keys.

"Hi, again," she heard that familiar deep voice
say. Darrin stood on the sidewalk.

"Hi," Deb responded.

He stepped closer, his scent wafting around her. It was different from last night—less spicy. And his features were softer in the sunlight. His chocolate skin seemed smoother, and she noticed that his nose, which was slightly pugged, jutted out. Deb let her eyes stray from his face to his mustard-colored single-breasted blazer. His broad shoulders were erect, clad in a cream silk shirt, open at the neck. Short, dark curly hair peeked at the crest of his chest. She ended her observation at his cuffed gray gabardine slacks resting just above his deep olive cap-toed shoes.

"I waited for you to come out of the restaurant. I hope you don't mind," Darrin said. "I wanted you to meet my sister."

The woman walked over to Deb and Darrin. She reached out for Deb's hand. For the first time since they entered the restaurant she could actually see that the young woman had the same smooth complexion, dark eyes, and soft features as Darrin. Deb dropped her keys.

"Sandra, this is Deb. Deb, this is my sister, Sandra."

"It's nice to meet you," the woman said. "Darrin told me all about how you tended to his wound."

"It was nothing, really." Deb blushed with embarrassment.

"Darrin, I have to go to the washroom. I'll be right back," said Sandra. "It was nice meeting you, Deb. I hope to see you again soon." She waved her hand and headed back to the restaurant.

Darrin watched his sister reenter the restaurant. "She's not fooling me. She saw some guy in there she claimed she knew."

"Big brother not approving?"

"Little brother, actually. And no, I don't approve. She doesn't know that guy. He could turn out to be like your former card partner."

They laughed. He stood there, towering over Deb. He held his hands behind his back.

"Wasn't that Denise with you?"

"Yeah. And her new date."

"You didn't look like you were having any fun. You should have called us over, I would have rescued you from the boredom. Besides, three's a crowd."

"And five just ain't allowed," Deb joked.

Darrin stepped toward Deb. "Denise and I had a long talk about you."

"Denise talks too much for her own good."

"Well, I was the one who asked about you after you left. You left so sudden I didn't get a chance to ask you for your phone number."

She looked away. She wasn't sure she wanted him to have her phone number. She just wasn't in the mood for any more games, in this lifetime or the next. Besides, Darrin could have any woman he wanted, so why would he want her? She tried desperately to think of some excuse not to give him her number. Before she could come up with anything, Darrin had pulled out a pen and his business card, so she just rattled off her number to him.

"Is it okay to call you tomorrow?"

"Sure."

"Great. I look forward to talking to you."

Sandra returned, escorted by some gorgeous guy, a smitten puppy-dog look on his face. Deb giggled.

Darrin frowned as he swooped down and picked up her keys. He opened the car door, took Deb by the hand and helped her into her Pathfinder. She rolled down the window. He leaned down, his arms resting on the door, his face just inches from hers. "Are you sure it's okay to call you?"

"Darrin, didn't I just say it was?"

"I just wanted to make sure. You know you really have beautiful eyes."

Deb blushed and turned away, pretending to search for something in the console. When she turned back, he hadn't moved. "Thank you," she said. "But mine aren't as dark as yours. Yours are almost black, they're so dark."

"Can you believe that they were gray when I was born?"

"Yes I can. My godson had gray eyes, and now his are a wonderful warm brown."

"Deb, I know I should have asked you this last night, and please forgive me for assuming, but are you dating, I mean serious like?"

She waited few moments before she answered. She watched the worried look stretch across his face.

"No, Darrin. I'm not seeing anyone...serious like," she mocked.

"I phrased that wrong. Are you seeing anyone, period?"

"No, I'm not. Why do you ask?"

"I was wondering...oh, never mind. I'll call you." And with that, Darrin tapped the side of the vehicle and walked away.

Deb could feel her cheeks heat again and she hurriedly started the engine. She looked at Sandra and waved.

Darrin turned and looked back. "I'll call you," he mouthed.

On the drive home, Deb recalled the scene between Darrin and his sister and smiled broadly. He was protective. She liked that.

Deb weaved her Pathfinder through the light traffic on the Dan Ryan Expressway. Her thoughts switched to other scenes: Darrin spilling the beer; the anger in his voice when he rescued her from her card partner; the warm, intense gaze in his dark eyes.

And she had given him her number. Somewhere deep, worry began to take over. What had she done? She wasn't sure she should have done that. She shrugged her shoulders. What's done is done.

Deb reached down to the floor of the vehicle and pulled out a case of cassettes. Without taking her eyes off the road, she grabbed one, flipped off its case and shoved it into the tape player. She punched the fast forward button until she found the song she was searching for. The music came out loud and sudden, the whole interior vibrating as the horn and bass track thumped. Deb felt soothed. The words from the song, "He's Just A Freak," by O'Bryan, helped some of her reserve return.

As she maneuvered the car onto the Garfield exit ramp, an idea hit her. She wondered why she hadn't thought of it before. And even though the idea wasn't fair, she decided to be conveniently busy when Darrin called.

✪ ✪ ✪

Shari and Rocket were on the porch when Deb pulled into the driveway. Rocket leaped from the porch, her tail wagging in wild circles as Deb got out.

"This dog is hilarious." Deb waved a bag of left-overs from the restaurant just inches from Rocket's nose. "Here you go girl." She placed the scraps on the ground. Rocket briefly glanced up at Deb before devouring the treat.

"I hear you one mean sister," Shari said as Deb stepped up on the porch.

"Denise must have called you."

"And how. She called me from Jon's cell phone and explained how angry you got when Jon mentioned your single status. You know, Deb, she was only trying to help."

"Help?" Deb's voice rose. "She made me sound like some lonely old woman desperately seeking a man."

"Come on, Deb," Shari began. "Do you always have to be so doggoned mean about everything? You just don't know when folks are in your corner—looking out for your best interest."

"Shari. She told a total stranger my business? Besides, what business is it of hers—or yours for that matter—whether I date or not?"

"Look, Deb, you don't have to get nasty with me. I was just stating the facts."

"How about you and Denise do me a favor: mind your own business."

Deb stomped across the porch, grabbed the screen door and paused only long enough to give Shari a full look at the seriousness in her face before she let the screen door slam with a loud bang.

"I can't believe those two," Deb continued her tirade as she climbed the stairs. "Always meddling in my life. I am tired of it. I'm a big girl. I can take care of myself. I don't need the Sorrow Sisters looking out for me or my heart."

Deb went into her home office, slammed the door, and turned on the stereo. She popped in the *Phantom of the Opera* CD, which she knew would irritate Shari, and turned up the volume full blast. She sat down in the large black leather chair her mom gave her two Christmases ago, their last one together, and closed her eyes. Though she tried hard to fight it, she continually saw Darrin standing on the sidewalk near the restaurant. Deb opened her eyes, shook her head, and moved slowly to the daybed on the other side of the room. She stretched out, closed her eyes again and fell into a fitful sleep. She dreamed of her mother.

Her mom stood in the doorway, her chestnut-colored face glowing in the sunlight that streamed through the blinds. She moved over to the daybed and sat down next to Deb, her hand gently stroked Deb's face. "Dear, what's the matter?" her mom asked in that calming voice of hers.

"I'm so unhappy, Mom. Why did you leave me?"

"Honey, I have never left you. I will never leave you," she said. "But, Deb, you should not be afraid to open your heart. You live by loving. Never forget that."

"But mom, I need you."

"And I am here. Just don't forget: you live by loving."

"I won't, mom, I won't," Deb said, stretching her arms out. She felt her mother's arms encircle her. A safe and warm feeling enveloped her, as her mom rocked her and hummed a soothing tune.

"I'll try, mom. I'll really try."

❍ ❍ ❍

The room was dark with the exception of the red indicator lights from the stereo and the screen saver of flying toasters on the computer monitor. Deb could hear Rocket whining and scratching at the closed door.

She rose from the daybed and sat in the chair. Rocket's scratches intensified. Deb reluctantly opened the door.

"Well, if it isn't the welcoming committee," Deb yawned at both Shari and the dog.

"Can we come in?"

Deb nodded her head and turned on the desk lamp, then sat back on the daybed. Shari stood silent.

Deb patted the space beside her. Rocket jumped on the bed and settled her large head into

Deb's lap. Shari's somber expression caused Deb to pat the other side of the bed.

"You know I love you like family. You're the only sister I have." Shari hugged Deb. Rocket sat up. She placed her large nose directly in Deb's face.

"You're family, too." Deb kissed the dog between her eyes.

"Deb, I'm sorry. Sometimes we think we know what's best for you and then we end up just making matters worse. Can you forgive me?"

"I'll forgive you if you promise to just let me handle this my way. Promise?"

"Promise," Shari agreed. "But let me say this one thing and then I'm through interfering. Deb, I believe Darrin likes you and he really wants to get to know you. You should give him a chance. If you don't open yourself up for love, then it will always escape you."

Shari looked at Deb and left the room.

"Maybe I should give him a chance. He's really not so bad," Deb said, as Rocket yawned loudly. "What you think, girl? Should I?"

Rocket whined. Her bushy tail thumped the bed.

"You know maybe I will give him a chance. Who knows?"

Chapter Four

From the shower, Deb could hear Rocket bark. Either someone was at the door or the telephone was ringing. She jumped out of the shower, grabbed a large terry cloth robe, and ran out into the hallway. The doorbell rang again, and she wondered who would be at the door so early on a Monday morning.

She hurried down the stairs, two at a time, Rocket fast behind her. Rocket barked wildly between low-throated growls.

"May I help you?" Deb peered around the door.

"I have a special delivery for Deborah Anderson," answered the delivery man.

"I'm Deborah Anderson."

"Please sign here."

She looked at the long white box curiously. It was wrapped in a big red silk ribbon, topped with a red bow. She opened the door wider and signed the registry.

Rocket's growls intensified as she stood between Deb and the delivery man. He stepped back, cautiously extended the box to Deb, then half ran, half walked off the porch.

"We must've scared him away," Deb said to the dog. "Me with this shower cap on my head and you with your mean growl."

Deb rubbed her hand over the box. Who could have sent it? She went upstairs and set the box on her bed. Rocket jumped up and began sniffing it while Deb merely looked at it. Curiosity was being displaced by a weary feeling as she remembered all the flowers Mario used to send after he got caught with another woman. Deb tossed the box into the corner, causing Rocket to whine.

"I know, girl, I should open it. At least to see who it's from." She picked up the box, sat down on the bed, and opened it. She read the hand-written card inside.

I couldn't decided whether I should call you first or send you flowers, so I did both. Darrin.

Deb turned around and noticed the red message light blinking on her answering machine. She walked over to the nightstand where the machine sat, pushed play and leaned back into the mountain of pillows on her bed.

Beep. "Deb, this is Shari, I will be home late tonight, I'm going out for drinks with Bruce after work. See ya. Say Rocket. Get off that bed!"

Rocket looked at the machine, turned her head to one side, and promptly jumped off the bed.

Beep. "Hi, Deb. I hope you like the flowers," Darrin's deep voice began, causing Deb to smile in

spite of herself. "Don't be mad at Shari for telling
me what your favorite flowers are. If you get a
chance, please call me at 555-6869. That's my
direct line. I'm looking forward to talking to you."

Deb's head began to spin and the following messages became a blur as she recorded Darrin's voice
in her head.

"Darrin," Deb whispered. "Darrin sent me the
flowers," she repeated as she carefully removed the
ribbon from the box to reveal bright purple and
white lilacs, white lilies, adorned with supple green
leaves and baby's breath. Deb pulled the flowers
close to her face, closed her eyes, and inhaled the
sweet scent of the mix.

For a moment, Deb swore she could feel Darrin's
hand on hers, causing a shiver to move deliberately up her arms, goose bumps rising. She placed the
flowers in a vase and sat them on her nightstand.
Images of Darrin's smile flooded her whole being,
spilling over and again. So much so, that she did-
n't hear the phone ring in her office until Rocket
began to bark.

Deb ran to answer it. "Hello."

"Hello, Deb?"

"Yes."

"This is Pat."

"Oh, hi, Pat, how are you? What can I do for
you?"

Patrick Petraski was Deb's editor at *Neighborhood Magazine.* For over a year, Deb wrote for the magazine and considered Pat a top-notch editor. Pat had always seemed to see the message in Deb's work, he had never tried to change her style, her unique voice.

They talked for over an hour about her potential feature story. Deb was thankful for the diversion. It gave her an opportunity to stall for time before she would have to call Darrin back, if nothing more than to thank him for the flowers.

"You need to come into the office tomorrow for a couple of hours," Pat insisted. "We also changed the schedule for the editorial meetings. We'll have them at nine instead of at two. Can you be here for that?"

"Sure, Pat, I'll see you tomorrow."

She sat at her computer and started working on her next story, calling contacts to set up interviews for the next couple of days. When she glanced at the clock on her desk, it read 11:30. She was already a full hour and a half behind her normal morning schedule.

The fragrance from the flowers in the adjoining room wafted toward her. The scent caused her to think of Darrin, and when she closed her eyes his voice filled her head, his full lips mouthing, "I'll call you."

He had a nice smile.

Deb walked out of her home office to her bedroom to retrieve the flowers. She returned, setting the heavy lead crystal vase on her desk next to her computer. Deb rested her chin in her hands, her elbows on the desk, as she stared at the flowers. The smell of Darrin's last scent was different, more masculine. She shook her head in an attempt to release thoughts of Darrin and focus on the story when the phone on her desk rang.

"Hello. This is Deb Anderson."

"Hello Deb Anderson, this is Darrin Wilson. I decided to call you. I hope you don't mind?"

"No, I don't mind."

"I can call back if you're busy."

"No, it's no problem. Oh, Darrin, thank you for the beautiful flowers. I know Denise gave you Shari's number and you talked to her."

"Yeah, I had to."

"She was the one who told you what my favorite flower are. It's okay, though."

"At first Shari wasn't going to tell me a thing. She said you'd kill her. So I had to bribe her. You know, make her an offer she couldn't refuse."

"What was the offer?"

"I promised her court-side tickets to the next Bulls game."

Deb gasped at the thought of Shari sitting in the stands, not knowing a thing about basketball but faking it the whole while, and nonetheless having a great time.

"Do you like basketball?"

"Yes, I do. But I like football better."

Deb and Darrin talked for over an hour. Easily going back and forth about sports—he said he had never met a woman who knew so much about it— to social issues and their respective jobs. Deb liked the sound of Darrin's voice, the way it deepened when he talked about something he was passionate about, and the flat tone he used when he was displeased. When they ended their conversation, Darrin paused.

"Deb? Would you like to go outside?" he stammered. "I mean—damn! Deb Anderson would you like to go out with me?"

"Why, yeah, sure. Where are you trying to take me?" Deb asked playfully.

"It won't be to a card party, that's for sure." Darrin laughed. "Can I surprise you?"

"I guess you can. Just as long as you promise to have me home by eleven. You know Mama Shari will have your hide."

"Deb?"

"Yes, Darrin?"

"Thanks for not being angry at Shari for giving me your number. Actually she gave it to me the night of the party, but she thought you might hang up on me. So I figured I needed to get it from you

myself. And still it took me until this morning to
get up enough nerve to call you when I really wanted to call you last night," Darrin rambled.

"Why, Darrin!" Deb feigned innocence. "I would-
n't have hung up on you. Why didn't you call me
last night?"

"Well, I didn't want to seem...umm...pushy?"

"Pushy? Well, maybe not pushy. Determined,
maybe, but pushy? Nah. We'll just leave it at determined."

"Deb, I am determined. I was determined to get
to know you from the moment I met you. So, I'll call
you in a couple of days and we can coordinate our
schedules. Is that okay?"

"That's fine, Darrin. I'll talk to you later."

"Bye, Deb."

She hung up the phone and watched the screen
saver of toasters with wings fly at warp speed
across her computer screen.

"Maybe it's time I take some of Mom and Shari's
advice and live a little," she said aloud. "It can't
hurt."

❂ ❂ ❂

Darrin twirled around in his office chair, a broad
smile stretched across his face.

"My, what brought this on?" Sofia asked.

"Just life. That's all. Just life. And right now it's getting better and better," Darrin beamed. He knew she'd been watching him and worrying since he broke up with Traci a year ago. Sofia had been his administrative assistant for nearly ten years, but she had always treated him as if he were her son. And that suited Darrin just fine.

Sofia eyed Darrin. She could see the sparkle in his eye. That fire at one time had all but gone out completely. She wanted to ask, but knew that it was unprofessional to pry into her boss's personal business. At least she knew "her" name and that made her relax as she sat across from him.

"Well, I'm glad to hear it, Mr. Wilson." She handed Darrin a stack of papers. "Here are the reports on the Driver deal. Mike says it's a go."

"Great." He flipped through the report. "You know, Sofia, I think I'll take the rest of the day off. Life is beautiful, isn't it?"

Chapter Five

The sun shone brightly through the cream sheers as Deb rolled over in bed, her hand stretched out, blindly searching for the alarm. Deb hit the snooze button, rolled over and buried her head in the pillow. Rocket sat near the bed placing her head on Deb's pillow, whining loudly.

"Go away girl." Deb pushed Rocket's head off the pillow. Rocket jumped on the bed and stood over Deb, licking her face and whining. Deb sat up.

"Has anyone ever told you that you need a doggie biscuit to take care of that breath?"

Rocket whined again as Deb plopped back into the pillows. Again, Rocket jumped over Deb, landing on the floor, and turning around a couple of times, this time placing her nose directly in Deb's face.

"Rocket, go bother Shari," Deb groaned as the alarm clocked buzzed again. She looked angrily at the clock and moved slowly out of bed. Rocket jumped excitedly back and forth from the bed to the floor and back to the bed.

"Okay, girl, I'm up. I'm up."

Deb glanced at the clock.

"Rocket, it's 6:30!"

Rocket sat on the bed, her ears perked straight up, her head cocked to the right. Deb reluctantly grabbed a pair of sweat pants, a T-shirt and Rocket's leash, still hanging on her door knob from their walk last night. Rocket ran close behind Deb as she walked grudgingly down the stairs. She grabbed her running shoes and opened the front door.

Seated on the top step of the porch, she turned her face toward the hot rising July sun, stretching her long arms. As she became warmer, light beads of sweat began to appear along her hairline.

Deb picked up the newspaper behind her and laid it out on the porch as she put on her shoes. She read the headlines and sucked her teeth in disgust, tossing the paper carelessly behind her.

"'Morning, Deb," said their neighbor, Ms. Johnson.

"Good morning, Ms. Johnson. How are you today?"

"Just blessed, dear, just blessed," Ms. Johnson sang. "Rocket's been in my garden again."

"I'm sorry, Ms. Johnson. I'll tie her up in the yard from now on." Deb looked down at Rocket. "Bad girl. In Ms. Johnson's tomatoes again, ugh?"

Deb and Shari couldn't figure out why Rocket loved Ms. Johnson's tomatoes. Every summer, for the past three years, she would jump over the fence and raid Ms. Johnson's prized tomatoes. No mat-

ter what she and Shari did, short of tying her up,
Rocket continued to eat the tomatoes.

Deb ran down the walk and out onto the tree-
lined sidewalk. Rocket ran steadily beside her.
She jogged at a slow pace so that she could seize
the opportunity to look longingly into people's windows. Hyde Park Boulevard was her favorite route.
Just about every apartment, house, and two-flat
had windows without curtains, which allowed her
to see various art and pictures on people's walls.

As the two ran toward the jogging path next to
Lake Michigan, Deb noticed that the bright morning sky was beginning to turn a blinding blue—the
sun so bright it seemed as if she were running
toward a mirage.

At the path, Deb released Rocket from her leash,
and the dog ran wild, dizzying circles around Deb
before turning her attention elsewhere.

Deb stretched, bent her legs at the knees and
pulled each one up to her chest. As she tried to
keep a watchful eye on Rocket, she found her mind
wandering to Darrin and their date tonight. She
couldn't remember the last time she had anticipat-
ed going out on a date.

Well, I once was excited about going out with
Mario.

Deb forced the image of Mario from her mind.
Rocket's sudden barking and growling caught her

attention, so she walked over to the dog standing at the foot of a tree.

"Girl, what are you barking at?" She looked up into the tree and spotted a squirrel sitting on a tree limb. Deb shook her head and began to jog away, calling out to Rocket, "C'mon girl, it's time to go home."

Rocket hesitated, looked toward Deb and then back to the squirrel, and then ran to catch up with Deb.

❂ ❂ ❂

"Deb, is that you?" Shari called out from the kitchen.

"Yeah. You know, Rocket's been in Ms. Johnson's tomatoes again?"

"Oh well, we'll just have to tie her up. I bought some organic tomatoes the other day, but again Rocket just turned her nose up. I guess she just likes Ms. Johnson's lovingly home-grown tomatoes." Shari laughed.

Shari sat in their kitchen and read her horoscope. The horoscopes and the movie section were the only parts of the newspaper she read. She claimed the horoscopes helped her start her mornings and the movie section helped her end her evenings.

"My horoscope said that I'll win friendship from people who once snubbed me."

Deb spied over Shari's shoulder. "What does my horoscope say?"

"You are going to meet a tall, dark and handsome man, who will sweep you off your feet."

"Very funny, Shari."

"Don't you have a date with Darrin tonight?"

"Yes, I do."

Deb braced herself for Shari's line of questioning. She knew there would be no less than a dozen. She took a coffee mug from the cabinet, poured some coffee, added cream and sugar, grabbed a bagel and sat down across from Shari.

"Do you know where you two are going?"

"He said it was a surprise."

"A surprise? How romantic. What are you going to wear?"

"I'm not sure."

"Please wear something sexy, we don't want to scare him off."

"How can I wear something sexy, when I don't know where I'm going?"

"Okay, but at least wear something that will get his attention." Shari got up from the table to place food in Rocket's dish.

"Rocket, nummy, num," Shari sang loudly.

Deb listened to Rocket run from somewhere in the house, her heavy paws making loud thumping noises on the carpet. Rocket slid across the tiled kitchen floor and stopped just short of her bowl. Deb and Shari laughed.

"Wear something to get his attention," Deb repeated as she looked at her roommate dressed in a large fuzzy pink robe, yellow hair rollers poking out from under a silk scarf, and a mud pack plastered all over her face. Deb snickered lowly at the sight, thinking that if she wore exactly what Shari had on she would get Darrin's attention for sure.

"Deb, I'm serious. Please wear something eye-catching."

"Shari, I will wear what I have. Thank you very much."

"Just trying to help. So, what do you think about Darrin?"

"What's there to think about?" Deb asked casually.

"Come on Deb, be serious. Do you like him?"

"It depends. Do you mean: do I like his face? His voice? His clothes?"

"Geez, you're impossible. One thing, though. Give him a chance, Deb. He's really nice. I mean, how many men go to the trouble of calling all over town to find lilacs, as well as give up fantastic seats to a Bulls game, just to be with a woman? Also, how many men will take the time to call a woman's friends to find out what she likes and dislikes? You tell me, Miss know-it-all, how many, ugh?"

Shari had a point, Deb agreed. The facts were there. Darrin had put forth a lot of effort. Deb had to admit it, Darrin piqued her curiosity.

Shari got up and stood over Deb and placed her hands protectively on Deb's shoulders. She bent slightly so that Deb could see the seriousness in her face.

"Deb, I just want you to live again, that's all. I know I promised to let you handle this your way and I won't interfere. I just want you to be happy. Mario is in the past."

Shari hugged Deb tightly, pressing her mud-caked face into Deb's and ran upstairs before Deb could protest. When Deb heard the sound of loud music and the closing of the bathroom door, she considered Shari's words. Maybe it was time to live a little and take a chance.

"Darrin's really not all that bad. And besides, all he wants to do is go out. It's not like he's trying to marry me or anything serious like that. What can it hurt?" Deb asked Rocket. She picked up the newspaper and read her horoscope aloud: "Take a chance on romance. A new love interest emerges."

✪ ✪ ✪

Darrin heard the phone over the sound of the shower. He rushed into his bedroom, then hesitated before picking it up.

"Mr. Wilson, it's Sofia."

"Yes, Sofia, is everything okay?"

"You be the judge."

Sofia told Darrin about a prospective deal that he and his long-time partner Mike had been working on for over a year. The same deal that Traci had insisted he and Mike get into. She had told them that overseas acquisitions were hot.

"Wait, Sofia, did you make reservations at the Hancock for two?"

"Yes, sir. All done."

Darrin sat on the edge of his bed, a towel wrapped about his narrow waist. He stroked his newly close cut hair.

"Mr. Jankowski called today. Seems as if he's having second thoughts about the overseas acquisitions."

"Did the final prospectus come in?"

"Yes, it arrived via messenger this morning."

"Okay, Sofia, tell Mike to call Jankowski and set up a meeting for first thing in the morning so he can show the prospectus. Once he sets up the meeting, call me."

Darrin hung up the phone. His company, Wilson & Associates, started as a simple computer software company that distributed software to small start-up companies with a shoestring budget. Darrin had always been proud of the relationships he had established with his customers and

only expanded when he saw that the need existed
for those same small companies. He had sewn up
the market with shrewd decisions and a flawless
marketing strategy. Five years later, Wilson &
Associates had become a leader in the software
field.

Darrin dried off as he walked to his closet. He
thought back to the night he met Deb. He studied
his hand as he absently rubbed it. Her hands were
smooth. He inhaled deeply—the scent of Deb filled
his nostrils and worked its way back into the
recesses of his mind. A strange and sudden feeling
snaked through his veins, and Darrin shivered
involuntarily.

It took him two hours to prepare for his date
with Deb. He looked in the mirror one last time
before he headed out the door. The phone ringing
stopped him.

✪ ✪ ✪

"Hurry up, Deb. Darrin will be here any moment."

"I am, I am," Deb screamed back at Shari. All
evening, Shari had dressed and undressed Deb,
picking and then discarding outfit after outfit.
Shari had made such a fuss that Deb wondered
just who was going on this date.

"Deb, why don't you wear a little makeup?"

"No thank you. I like the ugly look." Deb waved Shari away.

"Well, if you won't wear a little makeup, at least let me do something to your hair. It's a mess!"

"No, Shari. Now go away."

Shari threw her hands up in surrender, smiled and backed up to the wall to watch Deb finish dressing. Deb could see that Shari wanted to help and was having a hard time containing her comments, but Deb ignored the look, and settled for her friend's much welcomed silence. She glanced at her watch.

"Gosh, time has flown. Darrin will be here in a few minutes," Deb said with a sigh as she scanned the pile of clothes carelessly discarded across her bed. Skirts, blouses, stockings, undergarments, all lay helter skelter—when she suddenly remembered that Darrin said to "wear something casual."

❂ ❂ ❂

"Mr. Wilson, I know you're on your way out, but this is critical. The investors are calling. Mr. Jankowski's was the fourth call I've received in less than an hour. He wanted to speak with you. He refused to speak with Mike."

Darrin sat on a stool in his kitchen, his head in his hands as he listened to Sofia on the speaker phone. Of all the nights, this would be the one night things would go wrong. "Get him on the phone, then...conference him in."

Darrin paced the floor while he waited. He couldn't figure out why his investors would want to pull out just when the deal was nearly done.

"Mr. Wilson, I've got Mr. Jankowski on the phone."

Darrin spoke with Jankowski then one investor after another. He became worried. He didn't understand. Just last week they were all for investing in Wilson & Associates' plan to go global. Darrin knew that if they pulled out he'd be ruined. He paced faster. Every thought stopped him. He snapped his fingers.

"Sofia, are you there?"

"Yes, Mr. Wilson."

"Book me on the next thing smoking to New York out of O'Hare. I'm leaving now."

Darrin went to his room, threw some clothes into a garment bag, then grabbed his briefcase.

"Sofia, I should be back day after tomorrow. I'll call you later. See you in a couple of days."

❈ ❈ ❈

Deb decided on wearing a linen tunic and matching ankle length skirt.

"I don't like that," Shari bemoaned.

"Too bad. Besides, Darrin said to wear something casual."

"What you have on is too casual."

"You think so?" Deb tilted her head to one side as she studied her reflection in the mirror. Her dark brown eyes, sun-streaked hair, cocoa tone, and round tipped nose all stared back. "I'm cute in this outfit," Deb pep-talked.

"Here, wear these," Shari said from inside Deb's closet as she held up a pair of taupe linen shoes with a short heel. She tossed them over to Deb. "This makes you look stylish, grown up, but not too old. God, I wish you would stop cutting your hair." Shari raked her fingers through Deb's hair.

"Look, Shari, will you stop fussing over me. I'm a big girl, you know?"

"I know, but I want you to look fantabulous!"

Deb laughed at Shari's made-up-word, short for fantastic and fabulous, and looked back to the mirror, adding clear lip gloss followed by lipstick in a warm-red color. Deb pursed her lips, reeled back to get a full look at her face, patted her hair and then stood up. Now or never.

"Okay, girl, you good to go!" Shari said, beaming at Deb.

The phone rang. Shari and Deb looked curiously at each other, as Deb walked over to the phone.

"Hello?"

"Ms. Anderson?"

"Yes?"

"This is Mr. Wilson's secretary, Sofia. I'm afraid that Mr. Wilson will be unable to make it this evening. He had some very important business he had to take care of, which will take him out of town for a couple of days. He sends his sincere apologies."

"I see. Thank you for calling," Deb said into the receiver, then hung up the phone. She turned and looked in the mirror, her face blank. "Cancel? Darrin canceled," she mumbled as she sat on her bed then kicked off her shoes. "I knew it. I knew it was too good to be true."

"Who was that?" Shari asked.

Deb avoided Shari's knowing eyes as she sped round the room, from her dresser to her closet, picking up clothes, placing them on hangers, and putting her shoes back in boxes.

Shari moved in front of Deb, stopping her. "Who was that, Deb?"

"Darrin had to cancel," Deb said, her voice barely above a whisper. "That was his secretary."

"His secretary? He couldn't call himself?"

"Seems as if he had to go out of town on sudden business."

Shari's expression went from curiosity, to anger and resolve. Deb sensed the quick changes, turned away, and continued picking up items around her room. Shari sat on the bed . She stared at her feet before commenting.

"Oh Deb, I'm sorry." Shari's tone bordered on pity.

"I knew this was all too good to be true. How could he stand me up?" Deb began. "Who does he think he is? Nerve of him. And to add insult to injury, he had his secretary—his secretary, of all people—call me. I'm through Shari. Through."

Shari stood. "Wait, Deb. I bet there's an explanation. I'm sure he didn't cancel deliberately. I'm sure he didn't have a choice. Why don't you give him the chance to explain why he had to cancel. Give him that chance, will you?"

Deb reeled around. "Why, Shari? Tell me why I should give him a chance? Why should I even care. He's just like all the other men. I don't know why I even listen to you and Denise."

"Now, wait a minute, Deb. You're tripping. One time, and you're ready to just say to hell with it? You're something else, you know that?"

Deb glared at Shari, but her look didn't stop her friend.

"All men aren't Mario. When are you going to see that?" Shari asked.

"Well, what else am I suppose to do?" Deb sat on her bed.

Shari sat next to her. "Call him."

"Call him? He stood me up, remember."

"He canceled. There's a big difference. Call him and leave him a message."

"I can't do that. Are you crazy?"

"No. Let Darrin know you're disappointed, not angry."

"Who says I'm not angry."

"You're just disappointed, that's all. You should—"

The ringing phone stopped Shari. Deb looked at her, deciding to let it ring.

"Pick it up, Deb. It could be Darrin."

Deb tapped her foot on the floor. By the fourth ring she had bounded across the bed.

"Hello." Deb's tone was angry.

"May I speak to Deborah."

"Speaking."

"Oh, good its you. This is Sandra. Darrin's sister."

"Hi, Sandra, how are you?"

"I'm doing fine. Look, Darrin is really sorry for having to cancel at the last minute. Things got a little hairy with the business today, something about the investors. He had to fly out to New York to meet with them," Sandra explained.

Sandra went on tell her that Darrin had initially planned to call.

"He called me just as the flight was boarding and told me to call you, but I forgot. Then he called me from New York. Girl, Darrin really chewed me out when he found out I hadn't called you. He knew that secretary thing wasn't going to go over too well. Are you angry? Can you forgive me?"

"It's okay."

"No, it's not. Darrin doesn't do things like that. And of course he expects me to handle situations the same way he does. Which is another reason why Darrin flew out himself. He could have sent his partner, Mike, but he just doesn't trust anyone else to handle his business." She paused. "Darrin was really disappointed he couldn't see you tonight. Seems as if he had some really big plans. You know, I shouldn't be telling you this, but I have never known for him to be so excited about a date."

"Really?"

"Yeah. So can you forgive me for not calling you earlier and explaining this whole situation? Oh, and he said he will call you tonight."

"I told you, you're forgiven. Thanks a lot, Sandra. You take care. Bye."

Deb stood there, the phone cradled in the crux of her shoulder and chin. She stared at the flowers Darrin sent her. For a long time Deb stared at them, a little embarrassed at the way she'd behaved. She had accused Darrin of not only standing her up, but being a treacherous liar as well.

Deb rolled her eyes toward the ceiling and moved her head. The phone slipped from her shoulder. She returned it to its cradle, sat down hard in her chair and reached out to the flowers.

"God, am I crazy? I really don't know this man well enough to be disappointed," she said. "It ain't like we're serious or anything. It was just a friendly date. And dates sometimes are broken, but then again, his sister could be covering for him."

Deb nodded her head at that last thought. There were plenty of times she and Shari had covered for each other. She turned to Shari. "His sister confirmed the secretary's story. He's out of town on some business."

"Do you believe her?"

"I have no choice, now do I?" Deb looked sideways at Shari. "Hey, I'm going to bed. I'll see you in the morning."

She shut the door and stood in front of her full length mirror. She could see that all too familiar haunted look in her eyes, the one that seemed never to go away but stayed as a constant reminder of how she really felt. How she had felt all these months. Deb feared it must be what caused Shari and Denise to worry endlessly.

Would she ever get over the hurt Mario had inflicted? She was a grown woman. She knew and understood that not all men were like Mario. She knew, yet the sadness, the distrust, stayed locked deep inside her.

She had loved him so very much.

"Loving lets you live," she heard her mother say.

But why was she thinking about Mario and hurt and love now? She knew she was being silly. The past had nothing to do with one missed date.

She shrugged her shoulders, stepped out of her clothes, replaced them with her pink Snoopy nightshirt, and pushed Rocket to one side. She climbed wearily into bed. The silence in her room agitated her, so she flipped on the radio. As usual, her favorite urban contemporary station was into its nightly program of playing old love songs. But it was one song in particular that caused Deb to flinch. The slow music began to croon sweetly from the radio, a smooth synthesizer introduced "Let Me Put Love on Your Mind," by ConFunkShun.

She listened to the words. They agitated her. But something made her refuse to shut the radio off. The words seeped into her—finally, she settled. The song had told her what she needed to hear. That she couldn't hide behind fear.

At the song's end, Deb shut the radio off and picked up a book on her nightstand. She flipped through the pages. She found herself staring at the words. Her thoughts tumbled between Darrin's deep chocolate face and her mother's soothing voice telling her to "love and live."

Why can't I do it? Deb wondered. Why can't I just open up and believe?

Chapter Six

Deb stared out the window of her office at *Neighborhood Magazine* and watched it rain. For her, rain and the month of September went hand in hand when autumn reached Chicago. But she liked the colors of fall—deep yellow, red, and gold.

Her thoughts wandered to Darrin. It had been nearly two weeks since she got the phone call from his secretary and spoke to his sister. And she hadn't spoken to him. At this point, she was sure he had no intention of calling.

Then why was she so listless?

"Deb, there's a call on line two for you."

"Terri, can you take a message? I'm on deadline."

"Sure."

Deb continued to stare out the window. She watched the rain drops hit the glass and then roll quickly down.

"Deb, sorry to disturb you again, but the caller insists on speaking with you," Terri said.

"Okay, Terri, I'll take it," Deb said, irritated. "This better be good. I said that I was on deadline. I've got too much work to do. Why would Pat be so cruel as to put me in an office with such a wonderful view. I'll never get any work done."

Deb pressed the button near the flashing red light and picked up the receiver.

"This is Deb Anderson, how can I help you?"

"Hi there," a familiar voice said cautiously.

She inhaled deeply. What timing he had. As casually as possible, she said, "Yes. What can I do for you?"

"You can start by accepting my apology. I'm really sorry I haven't called before now. Things have been seriously tense around here."

Deb ignored his words and repeated, "What can I do for you?"

"That bad, huh?"

"What do you mean?" she answered indifferently.

"Look, I couldn't help breaking our date. I know it was tacky to have my secretary call you, but I was en route to O'Hare and I just couldn't think straight. I had asked Sandra to call. I knew she would forget. I know that wouldn't have been any better than the secretary's call. And besides, Deb, all I can say is, I'm sorry. I truly wasn't thinking straight."

Darrin continued to explain and apologize for fifteen minutes. Deb refused to respond with any more than a cursory "I see" before she interrupted him and informed him that she was on deadline.

"Have you eaten lunch yet?" Darrin said hurriedly.

"I don't do lunch on deadline days," Deb answered curtly.

"Deb? You don't believe me, do you?"

"As a matter of fact, no. First you chase my friends for information about me, then you bother me for my number, set me up for a date and then you get your secretary, your secretary, to cancel for you. And to add insult to injury, you wait nearly three weeks before calling with an explanation. Now, would you believe that yourself?"

Darrin chuckled nervously. "You have a point there. And to be honest, no, I wouldn't believe it either. I guess what I'm trying to say is...you have every right to be mad." Darrin let out a long sigh before going forward. "But at least give me the benefit of doubt. I have wanted to go out with you from the first time I laid eyes on you and since that night I have thought of nothing but you."

Even though Deb could hear the disappointment in Darrin's voice, she wasn't quite ready to forgive him.

"If I was on your mind so much, then why didn't you at least call?"

"I tried to call you. Your machine always answered and I figured if your machine is on, then you are not home or unavailable."

"You should have left a message."

"Please let me make it up to you. Let me show you how sorry I am."

"Darrin, I really have to go. Good-bye." She hung up.

Immediately, she regretted what she had done. Yes, she was annoyed with him. And no, she did not quite believe his explanations. But she liked him. She enjoyed his attention, liked the softness of his voice, the way it got deeper, more sensuous, when he became serious. And she would have loved to go to lunch with him.

But she had hung up on him. Why hadn't she given him a chance? She shrugged her shoulders and turned her chair around back to gazing out the window.

Why won't he leave me alone, Deb wondered. I was just fine before he came into my life.

After the most cursory of knocks, Pat walked in. He looked at her, the view of the lake, and raised a brow. "So, how's it going?"

"What?" She concentrated with some difficulty. "The new job or this story?"

He sat down. "Both. You've been a little detached lately. Is there anything wrong?"

"No, just got some things on my mind. Nothing to worry about. Nothing I can't handle."

"Okay. Well if you need to talk, Deb, you know my door is always open to you."

"Thanks, Pat."

"Say, are you finished editing that piece yet?"

"Almost."

"Well, let me let you get back to work. Remember, my door is always open."

"Thanks a lot, Pat. I'll remember that."

She forced her attention to the story. She was grateful that Pat thought enough of her writing to promote her to managing editor. She was pleased that he would allow her to continue to write stories—even though she wouldn't have the time to do so as frequently as before. She watched the words scroll down the screen. The pleading sound of Darrin's voice rang in her mind as he asked her to believe him, to give him another chance.

Is it that important? Deb wondered. Is going out with me really that important to him?

Deb picked up the phone and then slammed it down. "No, I won't call him," she said aloud. It didn't matter anyway, for she had thrown Darrin's number out a week ago. She would have to call information to get it.

She hesitated, then picked up the phone and dialed 4-1-1. She gave the name of Darrin's business and waited for the automated voice to give the number. Just as she began to write it down, her computer screen began blinking, then went pitch black. She banged on the side of the monitor and heard moans and curses from outside her door. The system was down.

"The computers are down," a voice outside Deb's door yelled angrily.

She looked at the number she had scrawled on the yellow legal pad near her computer. Again she picked the phone up and slammed it down. It beeped and startled her. Maybe Darrin had decided to ignore her childish antics and call back. But, no, it was the intercom indicator light, meaning the receptionist was buzzing her.

"Yes, Terri?"

"Pat said the computers will be down for the rest of the day, so he's allowing everyone to go home."

"Terri, what about the typesetters?"

"That's the downside. Pat asks that everyone be on deck at six o'clock sharp."

"Six o'clock? In the morning?"

"Yeah, six a.m. tomorrow morning. Hey, even I have to be here."

"Thanks, Terri." Deb hung up the phone and settled in her chair. "I guess that kills most of my day."

She gathered her things, all the while thinking of Darrin and the foolish way she had reacted to his apology.

She looked at the brass clock sitting on her desk and noticed that it was just past eleven a.m. There were a number of things she could be doing, like arranging her files. Instead, she decided to go shopping.

She picked up the phone and punched in Shari's number at Macy's. "Shari Thomas please," she said when the receptionist answered.

"Shari Thomas here. How can I help you?"

"You can start by saying you're free for lunch."

"Hey, Deb," Shari sang. "What? You're free for lunch on deadline day?"

"The computers are down and won't be back up until tomorrow morning. And the kicker is that all hands have to be on deck tomorrow at six a.m. to finish copy that has to go to print before the end of the day."

"Six a.m. God, that's early. I'm just rolling over for my next twenty winks at that hour."

"Yeah, tell me about it. So, are you free?"

"Deb, I wish I was. We have a new shipment of clothes coming in. Plus I need to be here for a distributors meeting this afternoon."

Deb sighed as she listened to Shari rattle off a list of things she had to do at work. She admired Shari's tenacity and her glamorous job. As a buyer for Macy's, Shari got the opportunity to travel around the world purchasing clothes for their women's career casual line.

"Well, since you're not free I'm going shopping. I could stand a new suit. But, lunch with you would have made me avoid spending money."

"I know that's right. Where're you going?"

"Maybe to Field's on State Street."

"Say, if you wind up in the neighborhood, stop by. Oh, Deb, I got a call from Darrin today. You know he's really sorry and feels badly for having to cancel on you at the last minute. You know things happen. Look at you. The computers went down and you are stuck with nothing to do. So, why won't you forgive and go out to lunch with him?"

"Shari..."

"Okay, okay. I'm out of it, but at least think about it. Here's his work number." Shari quickly rattled off the phone number. "Think about what I said. Bye sweetie, I'll see ya later."

"Bye, Shari." Deb hung up. Shari's idea wasn't half bad. Lunch with Darrin would be much better than trying on clothes. She pictured Darrin's smooth face and dark eyes. She grabbed her briefcase, stuffed her books and papers into it. She reached for the yellow legal pad, picked up the phone, and dialed Darrin's number.

"Wilson and Associates," a female voice answered.

"Darrin Wilson please," Deb said quickly.

"I'm afraid that Mr. Wilson is out of the office for the rest of the afternoon. May I take a message?"

"No...thank you. No message."

✪ ✪ ✪

The sidewalks along Michigan Avenue were packed
with people. Umbrellas darted up and down as
people briskly dodged and side-stepped each other.
Deb made her way to the curb to hail a cab.
Several empty cabs whizzed by before one stopped.
She jumped in and told the cabby to take her to
Marshall Field's.

"Which one?" the cabby asked in a thick
Jamaican accent.

"State Street."

The cab pulled quickly away from the curb, its
tires screeching and horns blaring behind it. The
cab was noticeably cold, and Deb pulled her trench
coat up around her neck.

Deb looked out the window at the dreary day as
the cabby honked and crawled his way down
Randolph. Even though the Field's at Water Tower
Place had been a favorite of Deb's since she was a
teen, she preferred the old stone and granite struc-
ture of the State Street store. She always felt a little bit of nostalgia when she looked at the clock at
the corner of State and Randolph, visible a block
away.

Locals said that the clock had been in the same
location since Field's opened over 100 years ago.
When Deb was a youngster, her mother would take
her and her brother to the State Street store every
year just before Christmas to see the elaborate win-

dow displays. Deb loved to watch the mechanical figures dressed brightly in reds and greens.

"Three twenty five," the cabby announced.

Deb looked up and saw she was in front of Marshall Fields. She pulled out a five dollar bill and waved her hand at the cabby when he began the ritual of searching for change. "Keep it," she said, and got out of the cab.

Once inside Field's, she headed for the escalator. A young couple walked hand in hand ahead of her. At the bottom of the escalator, they paused and kissed each other lightly on the lips. The young girl smiled sweetly and pointed to the jewelry counter to their far left. They walked over to the counter and gazed longingly into the display case.

"I like that one, honey," the young woman cooed. "It's so beautiful."

"Yeah, just like you," the young man responded and placed another kiss on her lips. They stood there looking at each other warmly.

Deb continued to walk toward the escalator, her steps slow, when she bumped into someone. A coat and several packages dropped to the floor. "Oh, I'm so sorry," she said as she bent down to pick up the packages, noticing the store names on them. One from Nieman Marcus, another from the GAP, and one from Macy's. As she picked up the packages she noticed the immense chocolate-brown hands reaching out for them. She let her eyes follow the hands up a jacket-clad muscular arm, to broad shoulders, before she finally saw his smooth, smiling face. It was Darrin Wilson.

"Well, nice bumping into you," he said, grinning broadly.

Deb stepped back. Darrin took her hand in his and encircled her waist with his free one, and smoothly propelled her out of the way of the steady flow of people.

"I thought you were on deadline?"

"I am," she began, her face red. "I mean...I was, but the computers went down and when they go down it's up to the techies to fiddle with it. They won't be back up until tomorrow."

"Well, I'd say that's a good omen."

"For whom?"

"For me. And since I see you are obviously free, would you mind helping me finish my shopping?" Darrin asked. "It's Sandra's birthday, and I can't think of a thing to get her."

Before she could respond, Darrin began again. "I think you could help me find something stylish for Sandra." He eyed Deb from head to toe. "From where I'm standing it looks as if your taste in clothing is simple, not over stated."

In spite of herself, she smiled at the compliment. She watched him eye her black wool slacks, matching silk mock turtle neck, and crimson blazer.

"And besides, Miss Anderson, it will also give me an excuse to take you to lunch."

Darrin's mouth moved so fast that she didn't have a chance to reply or object to his wishes. He maneuvered her toward the escalator, his hand still on her waist, and continued to chat endlessly.

"And you're probably wondering who all these packages are for. Well, one is for my aunt and uncle's 40th wedding anniversary. And this one is for my little cousin, who's away at college and, well...you get the idea. I am shopping for the whole family."

"Who? Your wife and children? Or your girlfriend?" Deb shot back. She felt his hand tense at the small of her back and she looked directly into his eyes. She was immediately sorry for her offhanded remark. It was obvious from the expression on his face that she had stung him with her words.

"I thought Denise told you," Darrin began evenly. "I have no children, though I want three or four someday. I'm not married nor do I have a girlfriend, steady or otherwise. I am very much single and interested in one person."

He moved closer, his chest pressing against her shoulder, his hand tense. She noticed his dark eyes turn serious as the lines in his forehead increased with his frown.

"I'm sorry, Darrin. It's really none of my business," she said, trying to erase the dejection that crept over his face. "Look, let's start over. Forget what I just said." She paused. "So tell me, what else did you buy?"

Darrin's smile returned, his hand relaxed, the tension ebbed away. She gave him her full attention while he showed her what he had bought. He beamed proudly at the crystal clock he bought for his aunt and uncle. She took in his smile, invited the warmth that emitted from his body, his words. In spite of herself, Deb was attracted to his boy-like excitement and infectious laugh.

She allowed his hand to remain protectively around her waist as he guided her through the store. Item after item, Darrin would pick it up, examine it closely, ask the clerk scores of questions and then waited for her approval or disapproval. He repeated this meticulous process several times until finally Deb took him by the hand and dragged him to the ladies accessories department. She pointed out a green and gold silk scarf and a gold scarf ring to match.

"Okay, now that's for Sandra. I sure hope you're finished. I have never seen a man shop so intensely before."

"I am a very intense person. You'll see."

"Well, can you show me this intensity another day? My feet hurt and I would love to sit down."

"Oh, Deb, I'm sorry. Why didn't you tell me sooner? I would have stopped shopping. I could have done this any day."

"You looked like you were having too much fun, interrogating the sales clerk and changing your mind a thousand times." Deb looked up at Darrin.

"You have good taste. I like the gift you picked out for Sandra. I think she's going to love it. And wait until I tell her that you were the one who chose it for her."

"I hope she likes it. Did you say it's for her birth-day?"

"Yeah, it's Saturday. My aunt is planning a birthday dinner, after which, Sandra's got big plans."

"When is your birthday?" Deb asked.

"June 30th. How about yours?"

"A day after yours. July 1st. Canadian Independence Day," she said.

Darrin's eyebrows rose. "Canadian Independence Day?"

Deb chuckled as she began to explain. "I know, most people don't know that, except Canadians of course. It's just a bit of useless trivia, that's all."

"No, it's not useless. Now I know when your birthday is and that is one more thing that I know about you. Are your feet still hurting?"

"Honestly? They're killing me. I'm not wearing my walking shoes. I took a cab here and planned on taking a cab home, so I left my 'shop till you drop' shoes at home. Besides, I'm really not a big shopper. I only do it when I absolutely have to."

"You know, if your feet hurt that bad I can rub them for you. Or better yet, I could carry you through the store." Darrin closed the space between them. His dark eyes bore into hers.

Deb cleared her throat. "Ah, a foot rub sounds better."

Darrin studied her face. He reached out and lightly brushed a strand of hair off of her forehead with the tips of his fingers. He wrapped his arms around her waist. She took a small step backward. He took a small step forward. She backed up again. He stepped forward again. The two stood there, near a rack of women's clothes. His eyes searched hers deeply, then his face moved closer and his mouth captured hers. She closed her eyes as she felt his full lips pressed against hers, the softness causing a slight moan to escape her. She opened her eyes. Reluctantly, she pulled away, releasing herself from his embrace. The charge was there, she felt it, like none other she had felt before. She needed to gain control, stop the feelings before they got started. His kiss left her wondering and wanting. She had to switch gears, head this off. She started to talk as if nothing had transpired between them.

"You know if you carry me through this store everyone will think we're crazy. How about we just go and get something to eat?"

Darrin nodded, but stayed silent. He watched her mouth move as they stepped onto the escalator. He stood on the step just below her. She became tense, but something in his silence was oddly comfortable. She couldn't recall ever feeling this comfortable with any man before. She searched his eyes. They relayed the same intense message they had since she met him.

Darrin cleared his throat. "Yeah, lunch is a great idea."

Chapter Seven

People stood lazily around, gazing and pointing to the various menus placed boldly above food stands. Darrin and Deb stood there, looking from one menu to the next, commenting on how everything seemed to sound good. After several minutes, they decided to try the Mexican Cantina.

A tall woman with a deep olive complexion escorted them to their seats. Again Darrin protectively held Deb around her waist. She began to get that same warm sensation, feeling it threaten to envelop her whole body. She watched him interact with the waitress, an air of power surrounding him as he spoke in even, deep tones that conveyed confidence. Cocky was something she had come to realize didn't apply to Darrin Wilson. Her face flushed as his hands moved smoothly from her waist to her hand when he pulled her chair out. She tried hard to contain her expressions, tried to keep Darrin from seeing what she knew was telltale signs that he was affecting her. She placed the menu up to her face.

"Now that's familiar," Darrin remarked.

"What's familiar?" She peered over the menu.

"You hiding behind a menu. What? You didn't think I noticed?" Darrin laughed. "You hid behind

that menu at The Retreat until the waitress almost
yanked it out of your hand."

Deb couldn't help but chuckle. "My, aren't we
awfully observant. And I wasn't hiding."

"Whatever you say," Darrin whispered and
leaned over the table. "It'll be our secret. But what
I don't understand is why you..." His voice trailed
off, a bemused look crossing his face. "Oh, now I
know. You didn't know Sandra was my sister.
Didn't Denise tell you?"

"Let's just say, Mr. Wilson, that I can be a little
stubborn sometimes."

"Tell me something I don't know."

She felt as if she could kick herself. Denise had
tried to tell her who Sandra was, but she wouldn't
hear it. Didn't want to hear it.

"Would you like something to drink?" Darrin
asked.

Deb was too embarrassed to do anything but
nod her head. She knew her futile attempt to avoid
his stare was childish. But it was stares just like
his that spoke of things hidden. Agendas planned.
Bad ones. A voice in her said otherwise, and she
wasn't sure she should listen to it, give in to the
feelings that coursed through her. A tingling sensation around her waist made her more aware. She
tried to analyze the feeling as it moved down her
back, reached around her, and left a sensuous

trace of light, hair-raising bumps on her thighs and legs.

Darrin signaled to the waitress.

"We would like to order drinks. I'll have a Tecante and the beautiful lady here will have...?" He looked to Deb.

"I'll take a White Russian, with Absolut." She laid the menu flat on the table. The waitress winked at her, with a promise to return soon with their drinks.

"You know it was meant for us to bump into each other today," Darrin began. "I know when you hung up you were thinking that this man is only playing with me, but I'm for real Deb. I'm serious. I want to get to know you. Spend some time with you." He reached out and placed his hand on hers.

"Here ya go! A Tecante for the gentleman and a White Russian for the lady." The waitress placed the drinks on the table.

"Thank you," Darrin said without looking up.

"Are you ready to order?" the waitress asked.

"Yes, we are," Darrin replied, his eyes still set on Deb.

"The lady will have?"

She looked up. "I will take a taco salad, sour cream on the side."

With his eyes still on Deb, Darrin said, "I will take a yes to you going out with me Friday night. And a tamale con quesadilla, with Spanish rice."

The waitress scribbled on her pad and rushed off.

"Deb, you have to know that I really want to see you again, because sitting here with you right now is just not enough for me. Will you go out with me?"

She studied him and without warning her mouth took over. She agreed to see him again. To place emphasis on her words, she leaned forward. He smiled at her movement, her face inches from his.

"You won't be sorry. I promise you. You won't be sorry."

"I hope not."

❂ ❂ ❂

For the rest of the lunch Darrin chatted endlessly about his family, his aunts who stepped in for his mother after her death. And though he adored and loved them, he admitted that they could be a little overprotective.

"At thirty-five, I don't feel as if I need to have all my dates scrutinized."

"Are they that bad?" Deb inquired.

"Let's just say they can be a bit much. Their hearts are in the right place, but their actions don't always make it seem so. Don't worry. They'll like you. But, actually, I don't care if they do or don't."

With that last statement, he knew he would make sure there would be no problems, not with this one—not this time. Nothing was going to stand in his way of having Deborah in his life. It was something in her, something about her, that made him want to be with her, protect her. There was a light, he felt, that had been dimmed but not entirely put out. The right man could replace the pain with trust—and he was the right man. He only had to convince her of that.

Darrin felt like a spy. He had asked Denise a lot more about Deb than he should have. He knew all about Mario, and all he could say to that was he was glad he was gone. He didn't mind a little competition, but he knew when a woman's heart was elsewhere it would be difficult to penetrate. But he was willing to try.

◉ ◉ ◉

Darrin and Deb sat talking in the restaurant for nearly three hours. She hadn't realized they had been there so long. But it was refreshing to listen to him talk about his family, his sister Sandra, whom he adored, his aunts, and the death of his mother. He even went on about his company, which he and his partner Mike, a childhood buddy, had created from scratch.

"Gosh, Darrin, look at the time!" She looked at her watch. "I really must be going. Besides, I haven't gotten any shopping done."

"I'm sorry, Deb. Really." He grinned and took her hand and kissed it. "Actually, to be honest, I'm not sorry for keeping you. I've really enjoyed this. It's been a long time since I've had this much fun just sitting and talking. I hope I didn't bore you."

"Not in the least. You're very animated, you know that?"

"I think I talk too much sometimes, but how else are people to get a flavor of you, get to know you if you don't talk? But I know I did all the talking."

"It's no problem." Deb rose. She was in no way sorry for their chance meeting. She couldn't think of any better way to get to know a person. Especially this one.

A slight dread swept over her. She was actually sorry to have to leave him, she was enjoying him. His eyes. His lips. Just being with him.

"This was a great impromptu meeting. So, I guess I'll be getting the rest of the family business on Friday?" Deb inquired.

Darrin stepped in beside her as they exited the restaurant. He still hadn't answered her question, so she let it go.

The warmth of his body next to hers was evident as they strolled through the store, not touching, but feeling each other's presence. When it came time to part, they paused, hesitated. She didn't want to see him go, and she got the same feeling from him.

"So, can I call you, say, like tonight?" he asked.

"Sure, Darrin, you can call me."

"I really enjoyed being with you, Deb. Thanks a lot. I'll talk to you later." He kissed her lightly on the lips.

Deb observed him, watched as every few steps he turned to look back at her. She noticed his steps were graceful yet confident as he maneuvered, coat, packages and all, around crowds of people. At the exit, Darrin paused, his snug fitting black jeans outlining the muscles from his waist down to his thighs, and pulled on his overcoat. Almost as if he felt Deb's stare, he turned once again and flashed a wide smile before disappearing through the revolving doors.

Deb blushed at being caught, and waved. She hummed as she allowed herself to realize that she might actually enjoy being with Darrin if she only gave it a chance. Just a chance was all that was needed.

Chapter Eight

The rustle of packages became a distraction as Deb stepped from the store out onto the sidewalk. She chided herself over the amount of money she had spent, arguing that she had really gone overboard with shopping. Two pairs of jeans, a new Seville suit, two silk blouses, ten pairs of Hanes stockings, which weren't on sale, and a cardigan sweater. Deb laughed and reminded herself of what Shari would say: "I bet the racks just called your name!"

A cold mist was in the air, and Deb struggled with her packages as she hailed a cab. She was surprised when the cabby jumped out and began assisting her with her packages. She gave him a warm smile, rattled off her address, and settled back into the murky gray worn-vinyl seats. Her mind coursed between Darrin's smile and his black jeans, to his smooth skin and dark eyes. She was so entranced that she hadn't noticed the cab taking the side streets to her home. She preferred the scenic route of Lake Shore Drive, though she knew at the height of rush hour it would be thick with cars and buses. Her light mood wanted the steel-gray clouds that hovered low over Lake Michigan, its matching gray water as it slapped against the rocks.

"Sir, could you please take Lake Shore Drive?"

The driver flashed her a mean glance. She
ignored it. Instead she turned her attention toward
the lake. The waves seemed to react in unison to
the clouds, rolling in and then out, in and then out.
Deb watched in fascination, the sight of the water
calming and assuring her. Sea gulls darted in and
out of the clouds, diving their white bills into the
murky water. A lone jogger, dressed in black, ran
alongside the lake, seemingly oblivious to the mag-
netic effect of the waves and the water.

The cab driver's loud voice, peppered with exple-
tives, snapped Deb out of her lake-induced trance
as cars began to back up near McFedrich Drive.
This time it was Deb who threw the cabby a mean
glance. He apologized and pointed to the radio in
the dashboard.

"Do you mind?" the driver asked as he turned
up the volume.

"No. That's Yanni. I like his music," she
answered, nodding her head. She was pleased with
the cabby's musical selection. It was soothing and
it seemed to boost her spirits up a notch. She was-
n't in the mood for heavy beats. The two hummed
along as Yanni's even strings saturated the whole
vehicle. Deb leaned her head back and closed her
eyes. Darrin appeared. He held her close to his
chest, a slight smile stretched across his face. He
moved his head closer and slightly parted his lips.

She wrapped her arms about the nape of his neck and invited his full lips to play with hers.

Deb's daydream came to an abrupt end with the sudden jerk of the cab. Her eyes opened in time to see the cab and another car jockey for the same lane.

"Please be careful."

"He saw my blinker," the cabby hissed. "He just didn't want me to get in front of him." Deb and the cabby both turned, angry expressions on their faces. Both shook their heads in unison.

Deb let her eyes wander back to the gray water beating against the rocks and she became almost sullen when the cab exited Lake Shore Drive at 57th Street and headed toward home. When the cabby pulled up into the driveway, she noticed a black BMW blocking the way.

Darrin's tall frame rested lazily on the wooden porch rail, one leg firmly on the porch, the other swinging out from his body. His solemn face changed to a brazen grin when he saw the cab. He rose from the rail and descended slowly from the porch to stand at the edge of the driveway.

"Do you know him?" asked the cab driver studying Deb in the rear view mirror, his voice laced with concern.

"Yeah, he's a friend of mine. It's okay."

Deb leaned over, paid the driver, tipped him an extra five for taking the scenic route. Before she

could get out, Darrin had opened the passenger
door, and began pulling out packages before placing his hand out for her to take.

"What are you doing here?"

"Since we parted, I had this sudden urge to see
you as well as give you this." He smiled. His dark
eyes twinkled as he handed Deb an umbrella.

"I had so much stuff I didn't even miss it. Thank
you. Wait. I don't remember giving you my address.
How did you know where I live?"

"Denise gave me your address. I hope you don't
mind?" He looked at his feet then slyly looked at
Deb.

"I'm going to have a talk with that woman just
before I shoot her."

"Don't be mad at Denise, I wore her down."

"With what, may I ask?"

"Front row tickets to an upcoming play."

"You have a way with tickets, don't you?" she
asked, head tilted slightly. Her eyes shamelessly
roamed over his broad shoulders and wide chest.
She noticed that he was wet.

"Why are your clothes wet?"

"It was pouring when I got here and my umbrella wouldn't open, and of course I forgot all about
yours. I was out of the car and all wet before I realized I had your umbrella right here in my hand.
Sounds crazy doesn't it?"

"Yeah, it does," Deb smiled. "Well, don't just stand there, let's get inside so you won't catch a cold."

Darrin moved close and Deb could smell the sweet mixture of cologne and sweat. "If I do, will you promise to take care of me?"

"It depends on how sick you get," she teased. "I'm not very good when it comes to colds."

He scrunched up his face. "I can't believe that. You fixed my wound very nicely, see?" He held up his hand, showing her the once bandaged wound. "It healed up quite nicely. Thanks to a wonderful nurse who took great care of me in my time of need."

Deb observed Darrin, his trench coat slung carelessly over his forearm, his black shirt and matching jeans stuck seductively to his arms, chest and thighs. She couldn't resist the temptation to let her eyes explore his whole body, especially his lips as he stood over her. She shook her head, trying to lose the sensuous thoughts that threatened to invade her mind.

Deb led Darrin to the porch and opened the door. Rocket jumped up and rested her front paws on Deb's shoulders and licked her face in earnest.

"Glad to see you too, girl." Deb pushed the dog off her.

Rocket moved around Darrin and sniffed.

"She's beautiful. Did I hear you call her Rocket?"

"Yeah, Shari and I gave her that name because when we call for her to come and eat, she races through the house like a rocket. It's actually kind of funny to watch."

"My mother didn't like dogs or cats, so Sandra and I never had more than fish for pets."

"Shari found her in the street, and she just grew on us."

"Well, she seems friendly enough. Do you think she would mind if I pet her?"

"No. Go ahead."

Rocket's tail wagged wildly as she pushed her head up against Darrin's hand. He squatted and stroked and scratched behind the animal's ears. Rocket panted and whined as her tail thumped noisily on the carpet.

"She is friendly." He continued to rub Rocket.

"Well, let me repay you for bringing me my umbrella. The least I can do is to help you dry off."

"Why thank you, I appreciate it. Oh, wait." Darrin stood. He wrestled a small package from his coat pocket. "Just a little something I picked up for you."

She hadn't noticed earlier when they were at Field's. She stood there, her mouth slightly open as she took the small box from his hands. Her hands trembled as she slowly removed the lid, pushing back the white tissue. She pulled out a Mikasa crystal ball.

"So you can always find me and know who I'm with." Darrin laughed.

She laughed with him, more out of embarrassment for her earlier off-handed remark. She took his hand in hers. Standing on tiptoes, she kissed him on the cheek. She purposely avoided kissing him on his lips. To do so seemed to be inviting danger.

"Thank you for the lovely gift. Now, every time I want to find you, all I have to do is look into this crystal ball?"

"Yup. And if you want me to come to you, all you have to do is rub it and call my name, and I'll come running."

They stood there for a moment, unsure of what to say next. No matter how hard she tried, Deb couldn't shake the developing attraction she had to Darrin. His warm voice, the way he stood, even the way her body reacted when she was next to him all made her feel woozy, almost out of control. She had never felt these emotions course through her body. To her it was like a tidal wave that continually built. She moved away from him quickly.

Deb cleared her throat and headed to the kitchen, calling for Rocket to follow. She led the dog through the kitchen to the side door. Rocket looked back to where Darrin stood, then looked up into the sky before she ran out into the yard.

"You don't have to stand. Please, have a seat," Deb called to Darrin.

"I'm wet. I don't want to mess up your furniture."

"Oh, that's right. Take off your shoes and follow me."

She peered around the kitchen wall and motioned for Darrin to follow her. He walked stiffly behind her, as they ascended the stairs. She pointed the office next to her bedroom. "You can go in there. I think I've got some clothes that should fit you."

"You always keep spare men's clothes around?"

Deb raised an eyebrow. I deserved that one, she thought. "My brother, Tony, comes and visits every summer," she explained, "and he always leaves something behind." Deb went into her room, pulled a box from inside her closet, held up a pair of sweat pants and a matching shirt, kicked the box back into the closet and shut the door. She returned to her office and handed him the clothes.

"This is from his last visit. When you've gotten out of those wet things, hand them to me and I'll put them in the steamer."

"You guys have a steamer, like the ones at the dry cleaners?"

"Yeah, Shari is into designing clothes, so this stuff is just a trick of her trade. Your clothes should be dry in about an hour."

"Can you make it three hours?" Darrin smiled as he leaned against the door jamb. He brushed a strand of hair out of Deb's face, his hand stroking her cheek. "You're really pretty, you know that? But then again, I'm sure you've been told that many times before."

She shuddered lightly and gave him a half smile. Where had she heard that before? Mario most certainly had told her how he thought she was the most beautiful girl in the world, but for all his compliments he still broke her heart.

She paused only long enough to pull the door shut between them. Outside, she stood and listened to the sounds of Darrin taking off his shirt, and then his pants. As hard as she tried, she couldn't keep her imagination in check. She found herself wondering how his long, muscular legs, his broad chest and massive arms would look minus the clothes.

"Umm." Deb shook her head again, thinking she needed to get a grip on her feelings.

Darrin partially opened the door and poked his head out. He handed her his clothes. "Here you go."

"This will be dry in no time." She tried not to peek through the crack. Still, she saw his bare shoulder, his taut muscles.

Darrin winked at her. Heat engulfed her face, but she winked back before she rushed to the basement.

What would Shari think if she came home and found a half naked man in our house? she wondered. She pulled the shirt close and inhaled. She liked the scent, Darrin's scent mingled with a spicy, strong cologne. This was the one to record in her memory, not the scent he wore the night they met. The one Mario wore.

She held the shirt close to her chest. The sound of footsteps on the stairs behind her brought her back to her senses. Quickly she arranged the shirt and jeans on a hanger and slammed the steamer door. "Your stuff will be ready in about an hour. Would you like something to drink?" She walked to the bar as Darrin inspected the basement.

"That would be nice, Deb. What do you have?" He stopped to look at the various pictures of Deb and Shari and their friends and family on the walls. She cringed when he stopped at one picture in particular. It was one she and Mario had taken at Navy Pier.

She wished she had removed that picture, had just taken it down and tossed it in the fireplace. She made a mental note to do just that as soon as Darrin left.

"What would you like? We have Ginger Ale, wine, or beer."

He walked over to the bar. "Let me have a beer. Maybe this time I won't drop it and cut myself." He didn't look her way. She could see his eyes set on the picture of her and Mario on the wall.

"I'll make sure you won't break it. I'll pour it in a paper cup." She heard him laugh as she reached above her head and grabbed a large plastic cup. "Will this do?"

"Yes," he responded.

She turned her back to him and felt his eyes on her as she maneuvered around the bar, opening the bottle, pouring the beer. When she turned around, he was watching her closely. She could have sworn she saw a look of uncertainty, which quickly disappeared.

Yeah, I've got to burn that picture, today.

When Darrin took the cup, his hand brushed lightly against her arm. His touch brought an involuntary shiver from her.

"Are you cold?" he queried.

"Just a little. Nothing to worry about though." She lied. There was plenty to worry about. One was her feelings. The sensations Darrin left when he touched her were sending chills throughout her whole body. And when she dared to look right into his dark eyes, a new feeling took over. It left her light-headed and confused. She didn't understand how a man she had just met a month ago, but had no real interaction with since they met, could cause

her to react the way she was. Yet, the more she
looked at him the more she wanted to be with him.

As Darrin sat silently and watched her, Deb
attempted to examine her feelings. But the more
she tried the more frustrated she became with herself, because her resolve to remain single was slowly but surely ebbing away.

"Was that a picture of your former boyfriend?"
The question came without warning.

She looked at him, straight in the eye. "Yes.
Why do you ask?"

"I was just wondering," he answered.

She waited for him to say more. Instead, he
stared at her. She thought she saw a strange
expression cross his face. Pity? Deb wasn't sure.
Whatever it was, she found the expression to be
somewhat soothing, calming. She lowered her eyes
and knew that eventually she would have to face
her emotions head on.

"You know, it's actually a little chilly down here,"
Deb lied again. "Would you like to go back
upstairs?"

"Whatever you want is fine with me." He flashed
a wide smile. There was a hidden meaning to his
words, she was sure of it.

She headed up the stairs. Darrin followed.
They stopped in the kitchen. She turned and faced
him. He rubbed his thumbs rhythmically up and
down her cheeks as he gazed into her eyes. She

could see the warmth in his eyes, the passion. She wasn't sure what to do next, but was frozen in place as Darrin's face came closer and closer, his lips parted slightly. He gently pulled her closer, one hand on her cheek the other resting at the small of her back. He lightly, deliberately, brushed his lips across hers. She responded by parting her lips. She couldn't believe it; she was inviting his kiss.

Her whole mind went blank as the warmth from his body, his mouth, took over. She pressed against him, sliding her arms around his neck so she could caress the base of his jet black hair. They explored each other's mouths, their tongues mingling, tasting, feeling. Deb became lost, unaware of time and space as she allowed him to stir feelings she once wanted guarded and hidden. She moaned, she was sure loudly, which only made Darrin kiss her with more intensity and passion than she had ever known.

The jangling ring of the phone broke their mounting passion. Deb smiled out of embarrassment when Darrin sighed, reluctantly releasing her from his arms.

"Hello," Deb answered, her breath coming in short spurts. She was sure her face was a brazen brown-red.

"Deb?" It was Shari. "What's wrong? Are you okay?"

"I'm fine, Shari." She allowed herself to breathe. "What's up?"

"Are you sure?"

"Yes, I'm sure," she replied a lot more impatiently than she meant to. The last thing she wanted was to have to answer to Shari's fifty-million questions.

"Okay, if you say so. Well anyway, I just called to tell you that Denise gave Darrin our address today."

"I know."

"Oh? You do? How do you know that?"

"Because Darrin is standing right here beside me," she replied. She turned her back to him. She wasn't sure if she could stand to see that look on his face, the passion in his eyes. But she was even more fearful of him seeing the look in her eyes. The receiver in her hand became increasingly moist as Darrin casually massaged her shoulders, his long fingers softly stroking her. She leaned her head against his chest, and the feel of his warm breath upon her neck made her reel. She stepped away.

"Well, you go girl!"

"It's not that kind of party." Deb straightened.

"Well, maybe you need to make it that kind of party." Shari laughed. "And seeing as how I won't be home tonight, you can. If you get my meaning?"

"You won't be home? Why?"

"Nah, I've got a special date with Bruce. He said he wanted to show me heaven. This should be a treat."

"You guys are seeing an awful lot of each other lately."

"Yeah, and it's nice. Hey, stop stalling and get back to Darrin. Where's he at?"

"Right here."

"He's standing near you? I mean close enough that you can smell him?"

"Yeah."

"Well, let me not stand in the way of progress."

"Shari," Deb exclaimed and laughed out loud.

"I know, that was bad. Look, I'll see you tomorrow. Bye sugar. Now don't do nothin' I wouldn't." Shari snickered and hung up.

Deb held on to the phone. Her mind raced. What led to all of this, she wondered. And where is all this going? "Okay, Shari, bye. See you later," she said to a dial tone. Shari had already hung up.

"Deb, I'm sorry if I was too forward," Darrin said, turning her to face him.

His black eyes were pleading. She thought he looked like a little boy who knew better but threw caution to the wind just to get what he wanted. Deb knew they had to move, had to get out of the close space. She stepped back. "No apologies necessary."

She watched as the smile came back into his eyes. Now what, she wondered. She couldn't come up with anything else to say or do that wouldn't lead them into another embrace. "Would you like to sit on the porch?" This was the one thing that maybe would calm their emotions, clear the air of the charged electricity that had surfaced between them.

Darrin's footsteps made soft noises upon the carpet as he walked behind her. When they reached the door, they both grabbed for door knob at the same time.

"Allow me." Darrin bowed.

"So chivalry is not dead after all?"

"No. Not for me at least." He held the door for her.

Outside, Deb heard Rocket whining and barking. She went around the yard and opened the gate. Rocket bounded past her directly to Darrin. As he sat in the swing, the dog placed her head in his lap so he could scratch her ears and head.

Seeing the man and the dog, n "natural" combination, gave Deb a warm feeling. Too warm for comfort. She concentrated on his bare feet sticking out of the bright red sweats. A giggle escaped her.

"Now what? What's so funny?"

"That red sweat suit is awfully bright, don't you think? I didn't think it was that bright." She began to laugh in earnest.

Darrin looked down at his outfit, then looked back at Deb before letting out a deep laugh. "I look like a stop sign. You wouldn't happen to have a pair of socks would you? My feet are cold."

"I'm sorry. What size do you wear?"

"Eleven."

"I think I can do better than that. I just bought my brother some Nike running shoes and socks. Guess what? You two wear the same size."

He gave her a sideways glance. "Are you sure you didn't buy this ensemble for some other man?"

"Wouldn't you like to know?" she said with a snicker.

"I already do."

A wicked smile crept over Deb's face as she ran into the house, letting the screen door slam behind her. She cringed at the loud sound, shaking her head as she bounded up the stairs to her room, taking the steps two by two. She grabbed the items from her closet and ran back outside to the porch.

"I'll buy your brother some new stuff. When's his birthday?" Darrin asked.

"Next week. I was going to ship them to him in Tennessee."

She handed him the shoes and socks and sat down next to him. She looked up at the sky and noticed that the once gray clouds had finally given way to billowy white ones resembling large pillows as they gathered and moved rapidly across the sky.

Rocket, lying at Darrin's feet, let out a long noisy yawn.

"Looks like someone is sleepy." Darrin pointed to Rocket.

Deb and Darrin sat, making smalltalk. She talked about the change in the weather; he talked about how green the grass looked. It proved to be an effort for Deb. She couldn't seem to shake the image of the kiss they shared. Thoughts continually invaded her mind and she swore she felt him shiver next to her at the same time as she did.

"It's a little chilly out here. Can we go back inside?" Darrin asked.

She stalled. She was afraid that once they were inside the possibility of another embrace could, would ensue.

Darrin stood up and walked over to the door. He opened the screen and allowed Deb, followed by Rocket, to enter first.

She headed for the kitchen, then quickly changed her mind and headed to the second level where the den was. She stopped at the stereo and looked at the clock on the wall. It was time for her favorite urban station to play old school slow songs. She cringed and switched quickly from the radio to the CD player. The soundtrack from the *Phantom of The Opera* would be much safer background music than slow, romantic songs.

"I liked that play," Darrin said as he sat on the love seat. Deb sat on the floor a few feet away from him.

"You saw that?" Her eyebrows rose.

"Yeah, I'm a big fan of Andrew Lloyd Webber."

"So am I."

This time their discussion flowed effortlessly as they discussed Webber's work and other types of music they both enjoyed—until Darrin moved from the couch and sat next to Deb on the floor.

"Do you mind?" he asked but did not wait for her response. She felt the touch of his shoulder as he leaned over her, examining her expansive collection of CD's. "You've got some collection here. How long have you been buying all this?"

"Ever since I was young. My mom exposed us to all types of music. Salsa, Jazz, even Rap when it first hit with the Sugar Hill Gang."

"Now, that's an original. How about Doo-Whap or Ray Charles?"

"Them too. We didn't have one particular music we liked or disliked. In our house we listened to it all."

"My aunt really didn't listen to much other than gospel. Sandra and I didn't hear secular music until we were nearly in high school. But when we did..."

Deb laughed. "Y'all ate it up. What did you listen to?"

"We listened to a lot of what was out then. My all time favorites are the Isley Brothers and Barry White."

"Why those two?"

"I liked the music, the arrangements, and the words. Besides, you could always slow dance."

She refused to respond to his last statement. Imagine being in those arms, she thought as she watched him going through her collection.

He pulled out a CD. "You mind," he asked.

She nodded, and he placed the disc in the player. He selected a track, then settled back onto the cushion. She knew the song. Knew it well. Barry White's "Never, Never Gonna give You Up." Actually, she liked the song. She smiled as Darrin began to sing to her, his deep voice came out clear and smooth, matching Barry White's deep baritone.

She couldn't remember the last time she had been serenaded. She liked it.

Darrin rose. "Dance with me, Deb."

She hesitated only briefly, then let him take her in his arms. They swayed together, their bodies close. She rested her head on his chest and listened to the rhythm of his heartbeat, his voice vibrating deep in his chest as he sang to her, his face nestled in her hair.

"Darrin, you have a nice voice."

"And you, Ms. Anderson, are a great dancer."

They continued to slow dance. She closed her eyes. The music and his voice soothed her—carried her away. She held him, her arms wrapped about his shoulders. She could feel his hands, one on the small of her back, slightly above her behind, the other holding her tightly about the waist. She could feel the strength of his body, his breath slow and rhythmic. Every part of her called out to him.

She wanted to remain in his arms like this forever.

She couldn't believe it. And she felt safe. She had never felt safe with Mario; there were always feelings about him, bad ones, that picked at her constantly. But in Darrin's arms, in his presence, she felt good, protected—but most of all she felt wanted. How could she feel this strong so soon?

They remained locked together in dance through several songs. Finally, the last track on the CD ended.

"I think I better go home now." Darrin's voice was husky. "My clothes should be dry."

"Well, yes. I think so."

"You think what? My clothes are dry or I should go home. Tell me Deb, what do you want?"

"I think...perhaps...both."

Darrin slowly let her go. She watched his eyes as they searched hers. "Are you going to answer my last question?"

"I don't think I can, Darrin."

"I can, but I'll save it." He bent, kissed her lightly on the lips, and left the room. When he returned,
he was dressed in his own clothes.

"Thanks again for today." He leaned on the door
jamb as he spoke, his arm raised above his head.
"Deb, I am really sorry for standing you up. It
couldn't be helped and I couldn't be more sorry.
But, I promise you, I will never stand you up again
and you'll see, I will make it up to you."

She could see he was sincere, his dark eyes told
her so. He walked over to her, drew her up from
the couch. His face became a blur as his lips
touched hers. A deep passion welled up somewhere deep inside her, this time more powerful
than before. She pulled herself away and tried to
force a smile, tried to hide her emotions. She was
sure her face told everything she felt at that
moment. She had to change the course, come up
with some words to move them past what was
emerging between them. He reluctantly released
her.

Deb cleared her throat. "The best way to make it
up to me is to take me to a Bears game."

Darrin smiled. "You got a deal. You know they're
playing in an exhibition game on Friday night and
it's supposed to be an Indian summer day."

"All right, it's a deal. Good seats, and you're forgiven."

Chapter Nine

Darrin sat in his car, his fingers drumming the steering wheel. This night he decided to park the car himself instead of using the valet service. He had never met a woman like Deb. Sure, he had dated plenty of women, but this one was different. She touched his senses, made him feel alive. Yeah, he almost blew it. But he wasn't sure how she would react. But now after he had seen her again he knew that she had to be his.

He thought about her ex-boyfriend. The man had really broken her heart. And he could see that she wasn't quite ready to trust. With the right man she could. And Darrin knew he was the right man for her.

He whistled as he walked through the lobby of the building where he lived. He liked the location, the liveliness of the street. Most of all he liked the romantic view his 22nd floor condo gave of Lake Michigan. He wanted to share that view with Deb.

He could hear his phone ring as he stepped off the elevator. There were only two condos to a floor and he liked that; it allowed for plenty of privacy and space.

"Hello."

There was no answer, just breathing.

"Hello," he said again, angry now. These obscene phone calls had been going on for over a month. He seriously considered changing his number.

The bright moon shone onto the glass table in the living room. Darrin walked to the window and looked out. He spotted a single shimmering star and wondered what Deb was doing right at that moment—her bright smile and warm caramel skin pulled him. He liked her. A lot.

Though he had just left her, he thought of calling, but changed his mind. He didn't want to push, just gently prod. He wanted her to run to him, not away from him. He wanted her to want him.

The phone rang again.

"Hello," he yelled.

"What's up, man?" Darrin's childhood friend and business partner, Mike, asked. "What's wrong?"

"I've been getting a lot of prank phone calls. People calling and saying nothing."

"Any idea who it may be?"

"No. And I don't want to guess it's Traci."

"I hear you. So, man, where you been? I've been calling you all day. Sofia said you left early."

"That I did. I had an impromptu date," Darrin replied.

"Really? With who, man?"

"This woman I met at Denise's party last month. We started a little rocky, but I think that's over with."

Darrin sat down on the sofa, his long legs extended before him. He and Mike were like brothers, and though they were the same age, he had always gone to Mike for advice.

"Good. See, you should have called her all along. That was weak, dude."

"Tell me about it, but it's over. We're going to the Bears game."

"With the family?" Mike quizzed.

"Yes. Why? You think it's too soon?"

"No. It's not that. It's them crazy aunts of yours."

"That's not a problem."

"If you say so. I like Aunt Corretta and Aunt Esther, but they can be a bit much. You think she's ready for that?"

"Mike, it's not if she's ready—it's more of 'they better be on their best behavior.' I'm going to call the two of them tonight. I don't want no drama. I think this is the one, Mike."

"Well, you don't say. How did you get an impromptu meeting with her today?"

"I ran into her, or should I say she ran into me. Literally." He pictured Deb's face. "I talked her into going shopping with me."

"Well, now that's a new one. I've got to try that one. What's her name again?"

"Deborah. Deborah Anderson."

"Her name sounds familiar."

"She writes for *Neighborhood Magazine*."

"Wow, I read an article she wrote on kids in the juvenile justice system. She damn near had me in tears."

Darrin talked to Mike about the picture he saw on the wall in Deb's basement.

"And you think you know him?"

"Mike, I'm almost sure that's the guy I saw Traci with last week."

"Does he look her type?"

"Not at all." Darrin looked out the window, his gaze following the outlines of boats along the lake. He scrunched up his face as he wondered what Traci could be up to now. He knew that she could be real devious when she wanted to, and their last conversation left him wondering about her.

"Well, this city is just too small," Mike commented. "So, when am I going to meet the famous Deb?"

"At the Bears game on Friday."

"This I'm looking forward to. You really like her, don't you?"

"Yes, Mike, I do."

"Wow, I haven't heard you say that in a long time brother. Good to hear it."

"Well, not all of us have been so lucky to find as good a wife as you."

Mike teased, "Some of us don't deserve a good woman like my Gina."

"Yeah, right. I do," Darrin replied. "Anyway, Mike, I got to go. By the way, are we still on for that meeting with the school board in the morning?"

"I had forgot all about that."

"It's at eight o'clock," Darrin reminded Mike. "And don't be late."

"I won't. See you in the morning. Later, man."

"Later."

Darrin looked upon the water. His thoughts were of Deb and the expression on her face when he had held her in his arms. He wasn't sure if it was fear or passion he saw. But he was sure of one thing. He was drawn to her. He had grown tired of dateless evenings, or dates spent with women who talked about how much they owned, how much they made, and how a brother had to financially "come correct," as one sister had put it.

He stood, stretched, and decided to go to bed. He resolved to call Deb on Friday. Besides, it was only a day away.

Chapter Ten

"I can't find a thing to wear." Deb sighed as she pushed and pulled clothes back and forth on the rack in her closet. For this date, Rocket was Deb's only consultant. Shari was out of town. For once she wished Shari was at home to lend her advice on what to wear. Deb nervously twisted her hair around her finger as she swiped hanger after hanger of clothes back and forth. She frowned at each garment.

"Shari, where are you when I need you?" Deb asked.

The phone rang. She stared at it, her heart beating rapidly in her chest.

"I guess I should answer it, huh Rocket?"

She finally answered it on the third ring. "Hello?"

"*Buon giorno*, my friend. What are you doing?" Shari sang.

"Shari! Girl, am I ever glad to hear from you."

"Okay, what's wrong?"

"My date with Darrin is this afternoon and I can't find a thing to wear."

"You guys are going to a Bears game, right?"

"Yeah."

"How about that outfit I gave you for your birthday? You know the one, the camel-colored leggings and brown ankle boots. And wear that white, oversized oxford and my tweed jacket. Guaranteed, you will be cute."

"Thanks, Shari. How's Rome?"

"It is simply beautiful. And the men. Simply gorgeous."

"I sure miss you, girl. I wish you were here."

"I miss you too, Sistergirlfriend. I'll be home tomorrow. Look, I'd love to chat witcha, but this international long distance ain't no joke, and it sure ain't the next best thing to being there. Get my meaning?"

"I hear you."

"You have a wonderful time with Darrin, okay?"

"I will. I haven't been to a Bears game in years."

"Umm, how romantic," Shari replied sarcastically.

"I like football and I think it's a perfect first date."

"If you say so. Put the phone to Rocket's ear."

Rocket cocked her head, barked wildly and ran out of the room.

"What did you say?" Deb asked.

"I said, 'Nummy, num, Rocket.' Did she run?"

"Yeah, she took out of here like she was on fire. Why you make that dog think she's about to eat?

You're crazy. Get off my phone." Deb laughed and hung up the phone.

Deb shook her head. Rocket came back into the room, head hung low, and jumped on the bed.

"Sorry Girl, no food. You ate already."

Rocket whined loudly and rested her head on her paws.

Deb pulled the outfit from her closet and laid the items on the bed. She applied eye shadow, liner, and mascara. She examined her handiwork. Her skin was smooth and even enough that she didn't need to wear foundation.

She ended her ritual with her favorite cologne. She hoped it wasn't too strong—but it was sexy, and that's what mattered.

At the full-length mirror, she stared at her reflection, admiring her wide hips, narrow waist, and small bust. The new ivory-colored bra and thigh-high panties shaped her well.

She dressed, and once more stepped in front of the mirror. She twirled from one side to the other, pleased at the outfit. It was her—casual cute. And she loved the way the brown leather ankle boots made the outfit seem stylish, yet appropriate for a football game.

"Damn, Shari, girl! You got good taste," Deb said.

She was searching for her house keys when the phone rang. Not again, she thought. Darrin

wouldn't stand me up again. She walked over to
the phone, picked it up, and took a deep breath.

"Hello?"

"Hey there beautiful, ready for our date?"

A wave of relief swept over her. "Why, yes I am."

"Good. Go look on your porch and I will see you
in ten minutes."

When she hung up, she had an ear-to-ear grin
on her face. She ran out of the room and down the
stairs, Rocket was fast behind her.

She opened the door. At the top of the porch sat
a half dozen pink and white balloons tied to a big
brown teddy bear. The card attached to the bear
read: "Here's to the beginning of forever."

Smiling, Deb picked up the bear and balloons.
As she reached for the screen door she heard a car
pull up into the driveway. She turned. Darrin was
stepping out of his midnight-black BMW. Dressed
in blue jeans, a white shirt and black cowboy boots,
he gave her a wide smile. Slowly, she walked
toward him. When she reached him, he leaned
over and placed a kiss on her cheek.

"We're almost twins today," Darrin commented.
"Are you sure you weren't watching me while I
dressed?"

"No, but it could be quite possible that you were
watching me."

His eyes took on a mischievous component. "I
hope you like the bear."

"I love him. How did you know?"

Darrin smirked. "Do you have to ask?"

"I should have known. One of those meddling girlfriends of mine." She smiled to take the sting out of her words. "Let me take the balloons inside and get my purse and keys."

Darrin accompanied her to the house. She ran upstairs, grabbed her belongings, and returned to see Rocket planted directly in front of Darrin.

"You take good care of the house while I'm gone. See ya, girl." Deb bent down to hug the dog. Rocket moved to sit squarely in front of the door, her thick tail thumping loudly on the floor.

"Girl, you've got to move." Rocket whined and reluctantly moved from in front of the door, only to sit facing it. Deb shook her head as she closed the door and said a silent prayer: Lord, please let this be the beginning of forever

"How long have you guys had her?"

"Who? Rocket?"

"Yeah, she seems so attached to you."

"That she is. We've had her for about two years now." She went on to explain how Shari had found the animal wandering around the neighborhood and brought it home. They had placed signs all over, searching for an owner, but when no one called to claim the dog, they kept her.

"She's a good dog. A little mischievous. She loves our neighbor's tomatoes. Other than that she's really good. Has good instincts too."

"How so? You mean about people?"

"She didn't like my ex."

She watched Darrin's eyebrows rise. He seemed pleased.

She allowed him to place his hand on her back as he escorted her to the car. He opened the door and assisted her into the cool charcoal-gray leather seat. He walked around to the drivers side and slid gracefully into the seat next to her. He smiled and winked at her as he started the engine. She studied his movements, his large hands firmly placed on the steering wheel, his face serious as he backed out of the driveway.

"Wait." Darrin stopped the car.

"What's wrong?"

"Put your seat belt on, please. I would hate to lose you."

"Yes, sir." She saluted his stern words and buckled her seat belt.

◉ ◉ ◉

Traffic on Lake Shore Drive crawled, scores of cars headed north to Soldier's Field—home of the Chicago Bears. The traffic jam gave Deb an opportunity to absorb the view and the warm breeze as it flowed through the sun roof. The thick traffic also gave them a chance to talk.

"You know, I didn't think you would go out with me," Darrin said matter-of-factly.

"I won't even ask why." She turned her body around in the seat. "Look, I'm really sorry I hung up on you. Shari says I can be awfully pigheaded at times."

"I thought about what you said, about the excuse and having my secretary call you. And you know what?"

"No, what?"

"I wouldn't have believed that one either. I'm a little embarrassed."

"Why?"

"It was a bit pretentious to have my secretary call. I had too much going on, and that isn't an excuse—but just the same, it was tacky."

"Okay, it was tacky," she agreed and touched him on his forearm. "But let's forget it. Deal?"

"Deal," he agreed, letting his fingers strum the steering wheel in time to the music streaming from the many speakers of the car's stereo system.

Deb glanced out the window. Greenish waves lurched up the beach and slammed against the nearby rocks. Water always seemed to calm and soothe her, and before long she had shut her eyes to allow herself to daydream. Of days spent at the beach. Of sea gulls diving in and out of the water as she tossed bits of bread to them. Of sitting on a rock at night, light from the moon rippling through the calm waves. The stars were so bright she felt if she reached up just high enough, she could touch the tip of one.

"It's beautiful, isn't it?" Darrin whispered.

She opened her eyes. "Yes. I love the lake, especially on days like this."

"You know, sometimes I sit on the rocks and wonder who's on the other side of the lake. Then there are times I just sit and think. I come up with really good ideas when I'm sitting by the lake. We should go to the lake before it gets too cold."

She shifted in her seat. "I don't believe I thanked you for the balloons and the bear. Did Denise also tell you that I like balloons as well?"

"As a matter of fact, she did." He smiled as he glanced slyly at her.

"These bribes of yours are getting expensive."

"It's more than worth it." Darrin turned up the volume on the stereo. "This is my favorite song," he said as Luther Vandross' "Wait For Love" began. They both became silent as they listened to Vandross' smooth, sweet voice croon out the words to the song.

Deb turned her attention back to the lake. She began to ponder the words of the song. A voice inside her told her that she had found what she had been searching for.

✪ ✪ ✪

Soldier Field was packed. Deb accepted Darrin's
hand and held it tightly while they walked up the
concrete plank leading into the stands. When they
passed the 10th row, she looked at Darrin. He
winked and walked them over to an usher, handing
over two tickets and an orange pass. The usher
smiled and escorted them to an elevator. Deb wondered where they were going. She looked at Darrin.
He looked away. Her curiosity was piqued.

The elevator crept upward, the indicator light
flashing with each passing floor. Finally, it stopped
and the doors slid open.

A magnificent view of Soldier Field and Lake
Michigan greeted Deb. She couldn't ever remember
seeing such an impressive sight. The lush green
turf of the playing field was bordered by white thick
lines, which separated the yards with big white
numbers. Her eyes were wide as she observed men
dart on and off the field, in what seemed to her as
last minute inspections.

The orange and blue seats were occupied with
people in varied Bears colors.

She switched her eyes from the playing field to
the lake. A few small boats sailed by. From this
view, the water looked a deep aqua blue.

She was in awe. She had never been in the sky boxes before. The last time she attended a game was in 1985 when her mother took her and her brother.

"Darrin, this is magnificent. Simply magnificent."

"Well, didn't you say you would forgive me if we had good seats?" Darrin asked, his dark eyes twinkling. "Now, do you forgive me?"

"I didn't expect sky box seats." She blushed. "So, I guess I have to forgive you."

"Say everybody, here's Darrin," said a tall, robust man dressed in a navy and orange Bears sweat shirt and matching baseball cap. Next to him stood another man, much younger than the first and a little shorter than Darrin. They took turns shaking Darrin's hand. The older pumped Darrin's hand wildly while he slapped him heartily on the back.

"Glad to see you, my boy." The man smiled at Deb. "Darrin, who's this lovely lady?"

"Deb, this here is my Uncle Virgil. And next to him is my partner, Mike. Y'all, this is Deb."

"Nice to meet you." Mike shook her hand.

"Same here. Sandra's told us all about you," Uncle Virgil said. "C'mon. Let me introduce you to the family."

Darrin's uncle took Deb by the hand and pulled
her toward a group of women. Darrin nodded. He
mouthed, "It's okay."

She went from seat to seat as Uncle Virgil introduced her to several of his friends and their wives.
Their last introduction was that of a group of
women clustered together. Among them was
Darrin's sister, Sandra. Uncle Virgil introduced
Deb to his wife, Coretta, and his sister-in-law,
Esther. Coretta studied Deb for a long time before
she patted the empty seat between herself and the
other woman.

"So, what do you do?" Coretta asked snippily.

"Excuse me?"

"Do, honey, do. As in work?"

"Oh, I'm a managing editor for *Neighborhood
Magazine.*"

"I subscribe to that magazine. Hey, Esther, this
here girl works for *Neighborhood Magazine*. Get
that!"

"She does?" Esther asked.

"Yeah, well that's what she says. I didn't even
know they had any coloreds working there. What's
your name again, girl?" Coretta narrowed her dark
eyes.

She couldn't believe Coretta's last statement.
Colored, she thought, hell, I ain't heard that one
used in a long time.

She let the woman's words sink. She wasn't sure she should even dignify the statement with a response. Before she could respond, Esther spoke again.

"What was that last girl's name Darrin use to go out with?" asked Esther. She leaned heavily on Deb's arm.

"I think it was Traci. A pretty little thing. I think she was a model. On the runways of New York and Paris," Coretta responded.

"No, she's a lawyer, Coretta. You're thinking about the other one."

"Oh, yes. You're right. A real smart girl that Traci. I wonder what happened between them?" Coretta inquired. She talked to her sister as if Deb were invisible. "They were so in love I just knew they were going to get married. You know, I liked her for our Darrin."

"Me, too," chimed Esther.

The two women continued their tirade, discussing Traci at length. They glanced at Deb between words. She sat between them, her anger rising around her shirt collar and creeping up her face. Small beads of sweat appeared at her hairline. She could tell the two women had sensed her anger. They intensified their conversation.

"Traci is a litigation lawyer, specializing in workman's compensation issues," said Coretta.

"Didn't you say that her family is, ah, well-off?" Esther asked.

Corretta looked directly at Deb. "Ah, dear, what does your family do?"

"They live," Deb snapped.

Corretta waved her hand. "Umm, yes. Anyway." She turned her attention back to Esther. "You know, our Darrin should not have let her get away. I mean she had everything, a penthouse over looking the lake, a nice car ..."

"What kind was it, Coretta?"

"I believe it's the same kind Darrin has. A BMW, yeah, a BMW. You know they bought them at the same time, except for Traci's is red. Shame they broke up. I thought for sure he was going to marry her," Corretta said.

Unbelievable. She couldn't believe they were in the middle of a discussion about Darrin's ex-girl-friend with her seated between them. Darrin had warned her. She just didn't think it would be this bad.

"Excuse me. I see a seat where the air isn't so thick and the company sparse." Deb stood. She pushed past Coretta and bumped into her legs. She didn't dare excuse herself. She didn't feel the need to.

She took in several short breaths in an attempt to control her anger. She stood at the opposite end of the sky box and looked out over the heads of the crowd below her, her arms folded defiantly over her chest.

Out of the corner of her eye, Deb could see that Darrin had been behind her the whole time.

She didn't dare look his way. The agitation, she was sure, showed on her face. Yet, the longer she stood, the more angry she became. She spied an empty seat near Mike and sat down.

"Never mind them," Mike said. "Their bark is worse than their bite."

"Those two should be on a leash."

Mike laughed. "That's a good one."

Darrin walked over.

"Is everything okay?" he asked.

"I'm fine," Deb retorted curtly.

"Give me a second. I've got some choice words for some wonderful women." Darrin marched over to his aunts.

She could see the tension in Darrin's body, his shoulders erect and squared, much like the night she met him when he came to her rescue. Deb noticed the first person to move was Sandra.

"I'm sorry about that." Sandra sat next to Deb. "But I'm not half as sorry as they're going to be. Darrin doesn't like for Aunt Cora to interfere in his affairs."

"And how." Mike shook his head.

Deb watched Darrin as he approached the two women. He towered over them, the exchange did-

n't appear pleasant. His face was a mixture of seriousness and anger as his mouth moved rapidly.

An eerie silence fell over the sky box. The only
voice that could be heard came from Darrin.

"Aunt Cora," he began. "I want you to know I
heard every word. And I'm not going to ever repeat
this again. Mind your own damn business. Or I
swear, you'll never lay eyes on me again."

Deb felt Sandra's body tense.

"Oh, that's not good," Sandra said.

"Are they always like that?" Deb asked.

"Only when they think Darrin is serious about
someone. But I've never heard him speak to them
like that either. As to that crap about Traci—lies.
All lies. Aunt Cora couldn't stand her. And Aunt
Esther didn't like her 'cause Cora didn't," Sandra
said.

Deb picked up a pair of binoculars. She had
had enough of the drama. She scanned the crowd,
an endless sea of faces, and then down the field to
the players.

Sandra nudged her. They watched Darrin and
his aunts step out into the hallway. Sandra wrung
her hands, a worried look sweeping her face.

"It can't be that bad. Can it?" Deb asked.

"We all know one thing, he expects us to be cordial to his girlfriend."

"Look, Sandra, it's not that serious. Besides, I
really don't care what your aunts think of me."

"I hear what you're saying. But, for the record, Deb, I like you. I liked you when Darrin first told me about you."

She turned away from Sandra. She wondered why Darrin's sister was telling her all of this.

Sandra nudged her arm. Darrin and his aunts had returned. It seemed he had resolved the issue with his aunts and it showed on his face when he pointed over to where Deb sat. The two women headed toward her.

"This ought to be good," Sandra said nervously.

"Dear, we are sorry if we insulted you," Coretta began. Deb thought she recognized a pained expression on her face. She continued and took Deb's hand in hers. "Deborah, we didn't mean no harm. Sometimes we are just a little too protective of our baby sister's boy. Do you accept our apologies?"

Esther stood next to Coretta and nodded her head in agreement while her eyes searched the ground. Deb stood and extended her hand. The two ladies smiled at her. She heard Sandra let out a deep sigh of relief.

"Apology accepted," Deb said.

The two women invited Deb to sit with them, but Darrin stepped between them.

He took Deb by the hand. "That's nice of you, but she's going to sit with me and Uncle Virgil."

❖ ❖ ❖

During half-time Deb took the opportunity to get a good look at both women, who, she assumed, were both in their late 50s.

Coretta, the eldest, was slightly plump, remnants of an hour-glass figure still present. Her eyes were the same deep endless pools of black as Darrin's and Sandra's. They accentuated her crown of salt and pepper hair. Deb loved the color of Coretta's hair, hoping that when, and if, she turned completely gray, hers would be as beautiful. Coretta's deep caramel hands were smooth and accentuated by neatly manicured long nails painted a warm bronze.

On each hand, Coretta wore several rings. Deb walked over to the two women and sat between them. She asked Coretta about the rings.

"This is my mother's ring." She proudly held out her right hand. "And this is my grandmother's ring. And this one? This one belonged to my baby sister, Darrin's mother." She removed the ring and showed it to Deb. It was a ruby marquis surrounded by diamond baguettes. "It will be given to the woman Darrin marries."

Deb smiled at Coretta before turning her attention to Esther. She thought that Esther, the middle sibling, was built a lot like Sandra. She was tall and leggy with an ample bust. Her shoulder-length hair was pulled away from her narrow face and held in a tight bun by a gold-toned hair clip. Though her eyes weren't the same deep black as Coretta's, they twinkled a lot like Darrin's when she laughed.

Esther's complexion was the same flawless smooth skin and the same deep chocolate as Darrin's. She seemed more like she was in her middle 30s than in her 50s.

☙ ☙ ☙

When the game ended, Coretta was the first to speak. "Dear, it was really nice meeting you." She held both of Deb's hands in hers. "I sincerely hope we see you again and that you can honestly forgive two old, over protective women who just want the best for our Darrin."

Coretta turned to join her husband, Virgil ,standing near the door. She stopped, turned back and pulled Deb into her arms. She hugged her tightly. Esther walked behind Corretta. She paused and then waved.

Chapter Eleven

Deb held Darrin's hand as they headed for the car.

"That was some game," Darrin mused. "I thought Minnesota was going to kill them had it not been for Hinton's fumble. I hope you're hungry?"

"Are you kidding? All that food you guys had. I couldn't eat another thing if I tried."

"But the night is still young."

"That's true."

"Well, since you aren't hungry, can I surprise you with something else?"

"Okay, magician, what is it this time? I mean the sky box seats were more than enough."

"You'll see." She could see he had a guess-if-you-can expression on his face as he assisted her into his car.

The street lights danced on the windshield as he maneuvered the car down North Michigan Avenue. Store windows whizzed by as Deb watched the displays in the window.

"Let's walk," Darrin said as he parked the car. He stepped out and opened the door for her. He caught her hand as she eased out of the car. Deb didn't protest when he continued holding her hand as they made their way back to Michigan Avenue where at each window they paused to discuss the displays.

"When I was a teenager, I used to take the El from the South Side to Adams and Wabash and then walk to Water Tower," Deb said. To her, those were days she wished for. A time when nothing seemed to matter. "I would walk on one side of the street going and then the other when I headed back to the El. I would pretend that I owned the store. Those were some really good days, really carefree. I actually miss those days."

She became silent, almost sullen. Her mood lightened when Darrin pulled her closer and draped his arm protectively around her shoulder. They walked in silence. Deb hadn't known silence this comfortable. She didn't feel the need to make up conversation. His presence said everything. Before she knew it, they were standing in front of Water Tower Place.

"Wanna go in? Do a little window shopping."

"Why not? See what kind of set up these merchants have for Christmas."

"Ain't it a little early for Christmas decorations?"

"Yeah, but these folks seem to think that putting up decorations in October will get people in the holiday shopping mood."

Darrin stood to one side. She entered the revolving doors. He stopped them. She tapped on the glass door, a mock look of panic on her face.

He shook his head. She put her gloved hands together and mouthed "please."

Darrin pushed the door. "I never could resist a pleading woman."

Christmas music played softly overhead. Their hands were entwined. Deb couldn't remember the last time she felt so calm, so safe. She would have missed this opportunity by being stubborn. She knew there was nothing wrong with Darrin. It was all in her mind.

She slowed when his hand slipped from hers. She turned to see that Darrin had stopped at a flower vendor and bought a single red rose. She took the rose from his hands, stood on her tiptoes, and kissed him lightly on the lips. She watched his expression. She was surprised at her boldness. Again, she had kissed him.

They lingered at each window, where they discussed how good or bad the display looked. When they came upon the F. A. O. Schwartz toy store they stood a long while and watched the small children in the store run around playing with toy after toy. Sounds of giddiness filtered out of the store.

"Come on, let's go inside and play." Darrin tugged at her hand.

She followed him into the store, laughing at the way he half skipped, half walked through the door and then headed straight for a train set at the base of a large Christmas tree. He pushed buttons and flipped levers that made the train roll forward, white smoke billowing from its tiny smokestack.

"Is that your husband, or should I say kid?" a small woman with stark white hair asked from behind.

"Oh, no. He's just a friend," Deb replied.

"Oh, I thought he was your husband," the woman said. She held the hand of a man who, Deb guessed, was her husband. She watched the elderly couple as they talked softly to each other. They began and ended their sentences with "honey" and "dear."

She smiled at the woman and politely excused herself. The words of endearment rang in her ears. They were too cute, and she wondered if she spent the rest of her life with a man like Darrin, would they still use soft words to address each other in their "golden years." Would they still love each other? She hadn't thought about being connected to the same person forever. She glanced at Darrin and tried to imagine how it would be to grow old with him. Too soon. It's too soon to be thinking like that, she told herself.

She left Darrin at the train set and wandered down aisle after aisle, until she spotted a doll which looked liked the one she had as a little girl. She carefully picked up the cocoa-faced doll. Her red-brown hair was full of ringlet curls. She held it out in front of her. The doll's red faux velvet dress, trimmed in white lace at the neck, stood out and around its fat brown legs. She embraced the doll, closed her eyes, and hugged it tightly like she did when she was a child.

"Is that your favorite toy?" Darrin's deep voice broke in.

She placed the doll back on the shelf.

"I had a doll that looked just like this one when I was a little girl." She sighed. "I named her Dolly Boo, but later, after a playmate said the name was stupid, I dropped the Boo and just called her Dolly."

"Whatever happened to her?"

"I let Dolly spend the night at a friend's house and I never saw her again. Sometimes I think of how crazy that was. She was my favorite doll."

"I had a favorite toy."

"Really, and what was it? GI Joe with the kung fu grip?"

"No. But what's wrong with GI Joe?"

"Nothing. You had a GI Joe?" She giggled at the thought of Darrin playing with GI Joe dolls.

"Don't forget the kung-fu grip," he replied.

"What happened to it?"

"I drowned him. His grip wasn't that good when it came to going down drains. He's probably float-ing somewhere in one of these seven great lakes."

"If GI Joe wasn't your favorite toy, then what was it?"

"It was Legos."

"Legos?" Her snickers gave way to laughter. "You mean those plastic things kids sit with and connect?"

He raised his eyebrows. "Yeah. What's so funny about that?"

"I'm sorry." She took his hand in hers. "I'm not laughing at the Legos, I'm laughing at the image of you sitting down trying to build something out of those. My brother had some and we could never make our Legos look like the pictures on the box."

"I know. I tried, but mine always turned out wrong. For the life of me, I never understood why I never got the ones with the wheels. Still, it was` my favorite."

She listened as he talked about the various toys he had growing up. He named train sets, racing cars, and bikes. She tried to picture him and his friends performing stunts as they rode recklessly through their neighborhood.

"We were nuts," he said. "Well, I've played enough in here. Come on, let's get some ice cream."

On the eighth floor they stopped at D. B. Kaplan's Deli and ordered a large chocolate milk-shake.

They talked endlessly about Darrin's company and his family. Her mind floated to the feel of his soft, full lips upon hers. She liked the way they moved when he talked. The more she watched him, the more she wanted to just reach over and kiss him—take his smooth face in her hands. She had to admit it, she liked Darrin.

Once they finished, they exited Water Tower Place and headed toward the John Hancock Building, where Darrin stopped a horse-drawn carriage. Deb stood on the sidewalk as he climbed into the carriage. He held out his hand to her.

"Would you do me the pleasure of an evening ride around the block?"

She settled into the carriage next to him. She tried to relax. Carriage rides were one of the most romantic things she should could think of. She used to try and get Mario to take her on one, but he would say they were too expensive and not for "black folks."

Darrin handed the female driver a twenty dollar bill and asked her to "take it real slow." The driver smiled and nodded her head.

The horse's hooves made a rhythmic sound on the concrete pavement as the driver steered the brown and tan mare into the light evening traffic and headed toward the outer drive of Lake Shore Drive.

"Actually, I can't wait for Christmas. It's one of my favorite times of the year," Darrin said as the carriage slowly passed store windows.

"Mine too," Deb responded. "What is it you like best about Christmas?"

"I like the way State Street and Michigan Avenue are decorated. When I was a kid, my mom would bring Sandra and me down here just to look at the decorations. She knew so much. She would explain the meaning behind each and every decoration. And if she didn't know, she would send us on a fact finding mission to find out."

"How did your mom die?"

"She died in a car accident when I was ten. Sandra was twelve. It was hard on us. She did everything. But my dad took it hardest," he said.

"How so. If you don't mind me prying?"

"Not at all. For over a year, he didn't leave the house. That's how Aunt Cora came to raise us. Mom was something else. She could cook anything. She could sew anything. And she always hugged us. She would stop what she was doing and give us her full attention."

His voice trailed off as he looked longingly at the windows.

He looked directly at her. "You remind me a lot of my mother, you know. You both are very definite about what you want." His voice was barely above a whisper. "What you will and will not accept from people. You're both very compassionate, you hate to see people hurting, but are fiercely protective of your own feelings."

She wasn't expecting him to see that in her—to read her so well.

"You didn't think I knew that, did you? I saw it in you the first time we met. I knew that somebody had broken your heart."

She didn't speak. He continued. "But Deb, the man that did it didn't see what I see. He couldn't possibly appreciate you the way I can. Deb, give in to your heart. You know you can only live by loving."

Where have I heard that before? She tried to ignore what she saw in his eyes. It was a passion she had never seen. She had seen lust, and she had seen fear, but the passion, the fire, was almost too good to be true. She couldn't deny it. Still she had her doubts.

She didn't want him to see she was falling for him, hard. Each time he touched her, looked into her eyes—even smiled at her, a little more of her reserve melted away. Like ice during a hot summer day, trickle by trickle, until it was a mere memory.

Darrin put his arm around her. His hand on her face. He turned her to face him.

"You know, Deb, I've been hurt too. Sometimes pain confuses you to the point where you run from anything good and you won't let yourself acknowledge that the feeling is right. I know what I'm feeling for you is right, Deb. Don't be afraid. Let me love you."

"Darrin, I don't know if I can." She freed herself. He gently pulled her back.

"You can love. It's all right to love. I won't hurt you. Deb, you're everything I've been searching for. How can I hurt what I so desperately want—what I so desperately need."

She was silent at his last word. The carriage moved slowly along the lakefront, the silence between them still comforting, even soothing. With Mario, silence always meant rage or pain.

"You are so beautiful, Deb," Darrin whispered.

He pulled her closer, his face a mere blur as it meshed into the darkness of the night. He slowly pulled away. Deb could see the harbor lights as they flickered in his eyes. He moved closer. And again he pulled her toward him. She felt his warm breath upon her lips.

"I don't ever want this moment to end, Deb," he breathed.

Their lips met and chills instantly engulfed Deb's entire body.

She shivered and let the kiss take over. Her mind twirled and tumbled. She hungrily returned his kiss. She put her arms about the nape of his neck. He pulled her closer.

They became lost.

She felt his hands move seductively up and down her back as she felt the weight of him against her breasts. She heard herself moan, somewhere deep from within, as his tongue began a skilled game and licked her lips smoothly. Then she felt it.

The fire, deep inside, had been ignited. She was lost and didn't want to be found.

Their trance was suddenly broken when the carriage came to an abrupt halt.

She cleared her throat. "I guess the ride is over."

"Our ride will never be over." He hugged her.

He handed the driver another twenty dollars, stepped out of the buggy and extended his hand to Deb. He stopped her and took a few steps back. He didn't say a word as he gazed upon her for a long moment. She felt the heat rush to her face.

She couldn't believe it. One date, a couple of long conversations, some flowers and balloons, and she had fallen for this man. She had to remind herself of her promise to protect her heart at all costs. But she couldn't deny the feelings Darrin had awakened in her.

Darrin's hands encircled Deb's waist as he lifted her out of the carriage. Her body slid slowly down the length of his as he set her on the sidewalk. They stood there. Her heart pounded heavily in her chest. He pulled her to him and kissed her wantonly. She tried to pull away, but he stopped her and held her tight against him. He rocked her gently from side to side. Only when the horse stomped a hoof and neighed loudly did they break their embrace.

"You are really beautiful. I don't want you to leave me yet. Would you like to go to Navy Pier with me?"

"Sure." Her voice was raspy.

He took her hand and walked back to the car. When he opened the car door and helped her in, he squatted down beside her.

"Does this night have to ever end, Deb? Couldn't you let me show you the stars each and every night?"

"Only if you promise to never take the stars from me, Darrin."

"I promise," he said and crossed his index finger over his heart. "Hope to die, stick a needle in my eye."

She nodded numbly. All she could think about was his arms around her and the fire in his kiss. As he closed the car door, Deb slid down into the coolness of the leather seat, put her head back, and closed her eyes.

Chapter Twelve

They walked along Navy Pier. She had to admit, she didn't want the date to end either. She wanted it to go on and on.

The bright lights from the harbor and the lamp posts along the pier added an air of romance as they strolled slowly hand in hand. The Pier was full of couples, some walked slowly, a few held hands. They watched other couples sit along the lake on old Victorian wrought-iron and wood benches and snuggle close as the moon cast a warm, but eerie glow upon the lake.

A flower vendor saw Darrin and Deb as they neared his cart full of fresh cut flowers.

"A flower for the lady," the vendor called out.

Deb frowned as she remembered that she had left her rose in the carriage. Darrin stopped at the cart. She could see the reflection of the moonlit water in his eyes and without saying a word he left her side and walked over to the vendor. When he returned, he had the vendor's complete stock of wildflowers, gazelles, and daisies in his hand.

"Flowers for the lady." Darrin bowed his head. She thanked him and deeply inhaled the sweet fragrance. She wrapped her arm about his waist as they continued to walk toward the end of the Pier.

"Let's sit here," Darrin whispered. "You know, you are even more beautiful in the moonlight."

"Flattery will get you no where."

"As you get to know me, Deb, you will realize that I don't say anything I don't mean."

She couldn't respond. He was saying and doing all the right things. Things she had longed to hear. And the electricity his body emitted, pure fire, was all she could think of as he sat close to her, his arm draped across her shoulders.

Behind them the waves had begun to slap the break wall harder and harder. She turned to see a yacht inching closer to the pier. People could be seen in the distance as they stood on its deck. Many of them were dressed in full evening attire.

As the sleek craft began to dock, Deb could make out its name on the forward bow: The Star of Chicago.

"Have you ever gone on the dinner cruise?" Darrin asked.

Deb frowned. "Only once."

"With whom? If you don't mind me asking."

"No. I don't mind. My ex-boyfriend, Mario. We went for my birthday. Just before we broke up."

"Did you enjoy it? I mean, you know," he stammered, then sighed loudly. "Well, you know most people get sick."

"Actually, Mario did get really sick. That put a damper on the whole evening. All through the cruise he was either in the bathroom or up on deck, so I missed dinner."

She could see that he was trying to contain his laughter. When she thought about how bad Mario had looked, his normally smooth caramel skin a yellow-green hue as he ran across the deck in search of a bathroom with his hand placed firmly over his mouth, she had to laugh, too.

"Did you really love him, Deb?" Darrin's voice was serious.

"I thought I did. We met in college and he was my first love. I thought we were made for each other. We had planned, or should I say, I had planned on marrying him. We even talked about having children. We had names picked out and everything."

"Why did the two of you break up?"

"Mario isn't the kind of man who believes that one woman is enough," she said. She paused and then continued. "So after his last affair, I was fed up. Besides that, my mom had gotten really sick and he was never there for me. You know what I mean? He couldn't support me. He wasn't accustomed to showing that kind of emotion. Wait. I'm just running my mouth. Why do you want to know?"

"I'm sorry if I am being intrusive. You don't have to talk about it if you don't want to. I was just curious."

"No apologies necessary, Darrin. I don't mind. It's just that most men don't want to know about former beaus."

"Well, I'm not the least bit intimidated if that's what you mean." He raised his eyebrows.

"No, I'm not implying that you are. My experience has been that most men don't like to hear about other men, especially from a woman they're interested in."

"So you know I'm interested in you. Finally the truth comes out." He faced her. "Look, Deb, I've been interested in you the moment I laid eyes on you. And then when we spoke, it was your quiet charm and unabashed humor that did it."

Deb chuckled. "I'm sorry about the sock and sandal thing."

"And hanging up on me?"

"I was angry, Darrin. I think you understand. As to the sock thing." She hunched her shoulders. "Well, I think you enjoyed my observation. You laughed. So, now lets call a truce. How about it?"

"Deal. For the record, I don't blame you for being mad at me. As to the sock thing? I went home and called Sandra and told her she was right. And you know what?"

"No. What?"

"After I told her all about you—"

She interrupted him. "You told her all about me? You don't know that much about me. What could you have possibly told her?"

"I told her that I met a girl—well, a woman—who is beautiful, smart, and funny. I also told her that you were the one who commented on my wearing socks with sandals."

"And what else did you tell her?"

"Do you really want to know?"

"Yes, I do."

"I told her that you were the one. The one I wanted to be with."

She walked over to the rail. Darrin followed.

"Deb, have you ever had the feeling that you've known someone forever?" He touched her arm. "I mean like when you first met Shari. Did you have the feeling that you had known Shari all of your life and were meant to be friends? Well, when I first met you, I had the feeling as if I had known you all my life. I felt comfortable. I didn't feel as if I needed to prove anything to you, other than my feelings."

"All this from one meeting?" she asked. She didn't want to believe that anyone could possess the kinds of feelings he was describing to her. After nearly six years with Mario, she just assumed that no man would tell her the truth.

"Yes, Deb, from just one meeting. I had to see you again. I had to prove to myself that I wasn't wrong."

"And what if I don't feel the same way?"

"I don't believe you," he stated. "This Mario, and I assume it was Mario who broke your heart, can't begin to understand the mistake he made in letting you get away. My mother always taught me that you should protect and cherish the things that are most important to you. And right now, getting to know you and being with you are most important to me."

Deb didn't move. She wasn't sure how to respond. He was everything she had wished Mario would be. But Darrin wasn't Mario. Far from it. And Darrin was saying exactly what she needed to hear. And she actually believed him. Or could it be that she wanted to believe him?

They faced the lake. Neither spoke. She felt his hand touch hers, their fingers entwining. It was comfortable. She didn't feel any tension, and he didn't pull away. He had laid his cards on the table, and it was up to her to accept the hand he had just dealt.

He broke the silence. "You see it?"

"Umm-hmm."

"Close your eyes and make a wish," Darrin commanded.

She complied and pointed her face toward the bright eastern star.

"Okay. What did you wish for?"

"I thought you weren't suppose to tell? It won't come true," she replied.

"No, Deb, it's the other way around. You tell and your wishes come true."

"Okay, then. You first."

"I wished that you will always be with me. Now you," he said.

Again his words silenced her. She couldn't find her voice. Couldn't find the words to tell him that she had wished for the exact same thing, except she had added a little prayer. She so wanted the warm, safe feelings to be real and not some dream that would soon turn into a nightmare.

She cringed at that last thought. She had once felt the same about Mario. Yet, being with Darrin, his emotions raw and open, she wasn't so sure anymore how she had felt about Mario.

"Deb, you don't have to tell me what you wished if you really don't want to," Darrin said.

She detected a hint of disappointment in his voice.

"No, Darrin, it's only fair. You told me your wish, now I'll tell you mine." She cleared her throat. "I wished for the same thing you did."

She could see from the expression in his eyes that it was now his turn to figure out if she had told the truth or was telling him what she thought he wanted to hear. She watched as his eyes grew darker. An uncertainty flickered in and out of them. It was the first time since they had met that Deb had seen him vulnerable. She felt his body tense. She lightly pulled her hand from his and faced him. She wanted him to see that she believed him, wanted him to know she felt the same. But how could she? How could she make him know that she had fallen for him?

"Let's walk," Darrin murmured and slipped away from her.

Fear rose in her throat. She began to frantically search for something to say. She became angry at herself. Maybe her eyes lied and showed a different emotion than the one she wanted him to see.

Oh, well, this is another failed attempt at dating, she thought. She was ready to end the night and began to walk quickly in order to catch up with him. She was stunned when he came to an abrupt halt, then turned quickly.

"Deb, did you mean what you just said?" he asked. "You didn't say that just because of what I said?"

"No, Darrin, I meant it."

She put her arm around his waist and began to walk.

They walked to the exit of the pier onto the bike path. Deb and Darrin walked and talked, laughter came easy to them. She was the first to notice that the sky had begun to turn a familiar tinge of orange, mixed with blue.

"It's 4:30 in the morning!" Deb said.

"So it is. Why don't we sit here on the bench and watch the sun come up? It's only about an hour away."

"Why not." She sat next to him on a nearby bench and snuggled against him, her head resting on his chest, his arm around her. She could hear the steady beat of his heart and feel the rhythmic rise and fall of his chest as he breathed deeply. She closed her eyes. He alternated between stroking her hair and kissing her on the top of her head. Her eyes opened slowly. He lifted her chin and gently pulled her face close to his. Their lips barely touched. His fingers softly stroked her face. This time she wanted to feel his lips touch hers. She met his lips with an intensity she didn't realize she had.

The chilling sensation was gradually replaced by a fire that wouldn't go out. It had her caught up in a passion that both warmed and engulfed. She couldn't control the passion. She didn't want to control it. The sensation made her feel as if she were floating.

"Where have you been?" he whispered. "I've searched for you, it seems all my life. Let me love you, Deb."

This time she kissed him and held his smooth face in her hands. She broke the kiss and replaced her lips with a finger. She began to trace a path with her finger, first across his cheeks, then across his neck, and ended at his massive chest. She placed small kisses on his cheeks, his lips and neck. Deb heard him moan, low and deep. And when she returned to his lips, he eagerly greeted her.

The night sky slowly turned to blue, and the crest of the sun could be seen as it broke through the dark clouds on the horizon's edge.

Darrin spoke first, his voice hushed. "I've waited all night for you to kiss me like that. You know that?"

"No. I didn't know that." Deb planted another kiss on his neck.

"Deb, you really shouldn't kiss me there." Darrin's voice was raspy.

"Why?"

"You just shouldn't."

She kissed him lightly on the lips. The fire in his eyes told her all she needed to know, all she wanted to know, and it frightened her. Doubt began to slowly creep into her mind and she stood up suddenly.

"You know, I've been gone all day and I really should be getting home. I know Rocket's lonely."

"Yeah, we should be going."

They rose from the bench. Hand in hand they walked back to the car.

❀ ❀ ❀

Deb felt a strange sadness when they pulled into her driveway.

"Darrin, I had a wonderful time."

"So did I, Deb. Thank you for agreeing to go out with me."

"No, thank you. The day was much more than I expected."

She stalled. She wanted to say more, but the words wouldn't come. She got out of the car.

"Deb? Can I call you later?"

"Sure."

"Then I'll talk to you soon. Okay?"

"Okay." Deb closed the car door.

Behind her, she heard the sound of a car door open. She turned to see Darrin lean against his car. He watched her walk up the porch steps. She waved to him. He waved back but didn't move. She waved again, this time more like a shoo than a good-bye. He imitated her. She laughed, opened her door and shut it behind her. Rocket sat at her feet as she placed her ear to the wooden door and listened for his car to start. When she heard the whine of the starter and the engine roar to life, she made her way upstairs to bed.

❀ ❀ ❀

Darrin turned on the radio, then quickly turned it off. He inhaled deeply. Deb's scent lingered and mingled with the smell of the leather interior. He closed his eyes for a moment, and her face flashed in his mind. He liked the way her soft brown hair hung just slightly over her expressive dark brown eyes. He couldn't remember ever meeting a woman with eyes like hers. How sad those eyes had looked the night he met her. It was what had drawn him to her.

I know I can erase that pain, he assured himself.

He continued to drive. He swore he could still feel the smooth touch of her hands as they stroked his face, the soft kiss from her lips. He revved the engine, throwing his car into high gear.

"Deb, you will be mine. It's only a matter of time."

Chapter Thirteen

Warm sunlight filtered through the partially closed vertical blinds as Deb blinked her eyes several times to adjust to the light. She rolled over and grabbed the alarm clock on her night stand.

"Twelve o clock? It can't be!" Deb sat upright. Then the memories began to flood her, like a frenzied sea that forced its waves against the shore. An all too familiar chill ran down her arms and a fire stirred deep in her body. She slumped back onto the pillows and remembered that just six hours earlier she was locked in a luscious embrace with Darrin Wilson, the sun rising over the blue-green waters of Lake Michigan.

She climbed out of bed and headed to the kitchen. Shari sat at the table.

"From the look on your face, I trust you had a wonderful night and morning?" Shari said. She inspected Deb closely as she walked into the kitchen.

Deb smirked at her friend and tried to ignore her knowing glances. She knew full well that Shari would not stop asking questions until she had all the information she was searching for.

"So? Where did you guys go after the game? What did the two of you do until well past six a.m.? Come on Deb, details. I want details."

"Shari, can I get a cup of coffee before we discuss my date with Darrin?"

Deb took her time and moved slowly around the kitchen. She knew that stalling would drive Shari insane. She enjoyed it.

"How can you keep me in such suspense? It's not everyday that my sistergirlfriend goes out on a date, stays out all night long and wakes up with a glowing smile. Now get real and sit down. I want to hear all about it."

Deb kept her face stone straight as she grabbed a cup from the kitchen cabinet and poured herself some coffee. She wanted to keep Shari in suspense. It was only fair payback for meddling, albeit good meddling. She wouldn't have ever gone out with Darrin had Shari not continually advocated on his behalf. She sat down and picked up the paper.

"Oh no, you won't." Shari snatched the paper out of her hand.

"If you must know, we went to the Bears game," Deb said. She studied her face. Shari was past explosion.

"That I know. And I know that ain't all. I know you guys did more than go to the Bears game."

"If you'd be quiet and let me finish!" Deb crossed her legs, took a sip of her coffee. She

chuckled at Shari, leaned over the table, her face
inches away. She decided that Shari had had
enough torture.

She went on to tell her all about the date, their
carriage ride, their walk along Navy Pier, and
Darrin's words of wanting to be with her. She
ended with, "Darrin was a perfect gentleman."

"Are you going to see him again?" Shari asked.

"Maybe," she answered coyly.

"Maybe? You better. Girl, are you mad? This
guy is wonderful and you are over here talking
about maybe! So, when's the next date?"

"I don't know. Darrin said he was going to call
me today."

"You better say yes to another date. Who knows?
Darrin could be the one."

"The one?"

"Yeah, the one you fall madly in love with and
marry, have some kids, and name your first daugh-
ter Shari." Her long eyelashes fluttered.

Shari's chatter faded and was quickly replaced
by Darrin's voice as he talked about his wanting to
spend the rest of his life with her. It just didn't
seem real to Deb. Actually, though, the idea of marrying a man like Darrin wasn't such a foregone one.
She liked him—really liked him. She liked the way
he walked, the way he smelled, his dark eyes. She
liked the way he held her tenderly in his arms and

the way his full, sensuous lips meshed with her own.

She would give him a chance.

◉ ◉ ◉

The warm water beaded and then rolled down Deb's hair and into her face. As she stood under the shower head, she swore she could feel his strong arms around her. The look on his face, the way the moonlit water danced in his eyes, and the way his body reacted to her kisses. The images refused to leave Deb. Instead they swirled around her.

"Deb, telephone," Shari said from the other side of the bathroom door.

"Who is it?"

"You know who it is. It's Darrin."

Deb grinned, turned off the water, grabbed a towel and wrapped it tightly around her. She paused and wiped the condensation from the mirror. The expression in her eyes was undeniable. She hadn't seen them smile in a long time. She had fallen for Darrin, this she knew. She resigned herself to take her feelings, their feelings, one day at a time.

Shari and Rocket stood in the hallway. Shari grinned as Deb brushed past them. She playfully swatted at Shari.

"Hello?"

"Hi there, beautiful. Did you sleep well?"

"Like a rock. I didn't get out of bed until well after noon. What about you?"

"I couldn't sleep. I thought of you all morning."

She wasn't sure how to respond. All of this was so new to her. She wanted give him what he was searching for. She understood the difficulty of searching for someone to be with, to love, to share your life with. Then she thought of her own needs. For a long time she had pushed her heart and feelings into the deep recesses of her mind. Now here was the dream and she didn't even know how to react.

Just be yourself and you'll be okay, an inner voice said.

"Deb? Are you still there?"

"Yes."

"Are you okay?"

"I'm fine. I want to thank you again for a wonderful evening. You were a perfect host and I really enjoyed your company, Darrin."

"You know we don't have to stop at just one date. If you don't mind, I would like to see you again."

A chill ran up Deb's arms and she broke out in a searing sweat. The words poured out before she could stop them. "It depends, Darrin. I'm really busy at work, and most weekends I play catch up."

"But you don't work all night. Let me take you out again."

"Maybe, I need—"

"You don't have to be afraid of me, Deb. I won't hurt you."

In her heart she knew what Darrin was saying was true. It was getting her mind in sync with her heart—that was another story altogether.

"So, how about tomorrow night? I've got tickets to a play and I need a date. Going alone is no fun," Darrin said.

"Well, you could take your sister."

"Oh, now that's no fun." He laughed. "Besides, Sandra is busy and I can't very well hug her all night. I love my sister, but come on."

"Then there are also other women. A nice looking man like you can't be dateless," she tested. She didn't recall him saying he wasn't dating anyone. She should have asked him that day at The Retreat.

Darrin sighed heavily. "I thought you and I settled that one. But, for the record, once again, I am not attached, seeing any one, I have no woman, girlfriend, lady, side buddy, nada. Now, will you go with me—and I won't be taking no for an answer."

"You won't."

"Nope."

"You sure?" she stalled.

"Positive."

She began to feel silly, the whole way she was acting began to wear thin. She decided it was now or never.

"Okay, what time?"

"Are you saying 'yes' to a date tomorrow?"

"Yes, I am and I pray I won't regret this."

"No, Deb, what I have planned for you, you will never regret. I'll be by to pick you up at six. Is that okay?"

"Yeah, six is fine. What should I wear?"

"What do you wear to work?"

"I normally wear business casual. I can't very well chase a story in heels." Deb laughed.

"That will be fine. See you tomorrow."

"Tomorrow. Bye, Darrin."

"Bye, Deb."

Shari was standing in the doorway when Deb hung up the phone. She refused to look at Shari, she knew the look that was going to be plastered all over her face. That "I told you so" expression Shari was so famous for. Deb jumped up and headed back to the bathroom. She closed the door and rested her back against it.

"You won't regret it," Darrin had said, confidently. But she wondered how could she be sure. That was all she wanted to know. How could she be sure.

Chapter Fourteen

For two months, Darrin and Deb saw each other just about every day. And in that time she had begun to know every part of his mind and he eagerly let her explore it. He could sense when she had doubts about his feelings for her; and even her feelings for him. His words would calm her. He would tell her that she had nothing to fear, all he wanted to do was to love her. He had gotten into the habit of picking up small presents for Deb, such as the music box that played "All I Ask," from *The Phantom of the Opera*, and the doll she held in her arms at the toy store during their first date.

Then there were the surprises. Like the day he invited her to have dinner at his condo. Deb knew that eventually they would take their relationship to a higher level. No matter what, she wasn't prepared, but she knew she wouldn't run either.

❖ ❖ ❖

At work Deb was at the end of her deadline when Darrin called. She had thought of him most of the day, especially after he called to tell her he had a surprise for her. He had been telling her for two weeks that she was afraid of seeing his condo. So on this night he insisted that they have dinner at his place.

"You know you've been avoiding my place."

"No, I haven't," Deb said. She realized that his words were true. It wasn't that she didn't want to see his place, it was that she was afraid of what would happen once she got there.

"So, how 'bout it? You game? Or, are you afraid to see the beautiful view of the lake?"

"I'm not afraid! And to prove it to you, what time will you be here? I can be ready in ten minutes. How's that for fear?"

"Wow, talk about fearless. I'll see you in ten then."

She hung up the phone. She wondered how it would feel for Darrin to take her, to quell the near uncontrollable surge of passion that grew every time she thought of him, got near him. Deb hit an orange button on her computer, sending the story to the typesetters, and exited the system. She got her coat, checked her hair in the mirror near the door, then rushed out of the office.

"See ya Monday, Toni. You have a good weekend."

"See ya Deb, and tell Darrin I said, 'Hi'." Toni smiled. Deb whisked past her, the papers on Toni's desk flew to the floor.

She stepped into the elevator, checked her reflection again. Lipstick. She realized she hadn't put on lipstick. She pulled it out of her purse, applied the glossy mauve color, and pursed her lips together. She sprayed some cologne between her breasts, lightly raked her fingers through her hair, then stepped off the elevator. She had a feeling, deep down, that after tonight her and Darrin's relationship would never be the same.

"Goodnight, Joe. Have a good weekend." Deb waved to the security guard.

"Same to you, Ms. Anderson."

She glided through the revolving doors. Darrin sat on the hood of his car.

"My, you're prompt."

"It's because I couldn't wait to see you." Darrin kissed her on the lips.

"Darrin, you just saw me yesterday."

"And?"

"And you're going to get tired of seeing me all the time. Don't you want to miss me?"

"Never," he responded. He kissed her again.

She stroked the side of his face.

He opened the passenger door, waited until Deb was safely in, then shut the door. He walked around and joined Deb in the seat next to her. He smiled at her and tilted his head backward toward the package in the rear seat.

"What's that, Darrin? It smells good."

"Ribs from Carson's"

"How did you know I had a taste for ribs? I don't recall telling you what I wanted for dinner."

"I guessed, and I see I guessed right."

"Okay, so now you get an extra brownie point." Deb pointed her finger in the air, making a notch on an imaginary tally sheet. Darrin laughed as he started up the car, made a U-turn, and headed to his condo.

✪ ✪ ✪

"Good evening, Mr. Wilson," said the doorman. He held the car door and put his hand out to assist Deb out of the car.

"Good evening, Mr. Johnson. How are you today?" answered Darrin.

"I'm just fine. Great weather we're having."

"Yes, sir. It sure is. It's a little cold for me, though." Darrin took Deb by the arm and escorted her into his building.

She adored the interior of the lobby. She commented that it looked like something lifted right out of *Better Homes and Gardens.*

On both sides of the lobby, the walls were painted a pale mint green. Several scenes of sea shores, painted in bright water colors, hung on the walls. The floor was covered in plush hunter green carpet, which played off the green and gold specks in the cream-colored sofa and matching chairs. The chairs and sofa were divided by a large, oblong cherry-veneer Queen Anne coffee table.

The elevator was at the end of a long corridor. Deb began to make idle conversation about the interior while they waited for the elevator to arrive. They stepped on the elevator and Darrin reached over her head and pressed the floor indicator. She was pleased when he pressed the button for the twenty-second floor. As the elevator climbed, he lightly stroked her face.

"Where have you been all my life?" he asked, his voice soft. She faced him and placed her arms around his waist. He kissed her on the forehead. She leaned her head against his chest. She had become accustomed to the sound of his heartbeat, but this time it beat slightly faster than it normally did. She knew he was nervous, and this caused her to become nervous as well.

They stepped off the elevator and Deb followed him down the long corridor. There were only two doors, one on each side. Darrin motioned to his right, placed his key into the lock, swung open the door, then stepped back.

She gasped loudly as she stepped into the foyer of the condo.

"I moved here about a year ago. I pretty much had the same reaction when I first saw the view. It's what sold me on the place."

A tall brass lamp, turned low, cast a warm glow across the entire living room. Deb stood still and stared over at the large picture window, which began at the ceiling and ended at the floor. Light from the moon pitched a warm glow throughout the expansive living room.

Near the picture window sat a beige chaise lounge with a brass magazine rack filled with papers and magazines next to it. Adjacent to the chaise was a large, overstuffed teal-colored couch with piles of pastel-tinted pillows carelessly thrown upon it. A statue of an African elephant sat next to the couch, and Deb could see a glass and brass table in front of it. On the other side of the chaise were several oversized pillows, piled lazily at the base of the picture window.

"Come on in and have a seat. Would you care for something to drink?" Darrin asked. He moved around her, stepped into the living room, and turned on the stereo. "Come on, I won't bite."

"I'd like some wine, if you have any," Deb said. She walked across the carpet and onto highly polished hardwood floors. Her boot heels echoed loudly as she slowly made her way to stand in front of the window. She stood there, mesmerized by the moon as she watched it cast a hazy reflection off the lake. She knew it would be wonderful to wake up to sun in your living room in the morning and fall sleep to the moon at night.

"Some nights, Deb, the moon is so bright, I don't even turn on the lights. And in the morning, the view is spectacular. You must come and see it sometime." He stood behind her and handed her a glass of wine. She could smell the scent of the cologne she had bought him as a gift. She was pleased that she had been able to surprise him, he hadn't expected it. It was one of her favorite scents, Alfred Sung for Men. Now the heavy scent had become intoxicating, causing her mind to reel. Her body stiffened in reaction to Darrin's closeness. He placed his hands on her shoulders. They remained silent as they looked out over the lake.

Deb needed to move. She knew that if she didn't, she would lose all composure. She faced him; the light from the moon shone in his dark eyes. She brushed slightly against his chest as she made her way to the large pile of pillows on the floor. Darrin walked to the stereo, put in a CD and adjusted the volume. Luther's "Never Too Much" crooned out of a set of speakers overhead. He returned to the window. She could sense the electricity charging from his body, and it clung in the air like lightning during a storm. He turned to face her. The look he gave her was the same one she had witnessed the first time they kissed, really kissed, in the carriage.

He left the window and walked toward her.

"Do you mind?" Darrin pointed next to Deb.

"No. Please sit." She patted the empty space next to her on the pillows.

His body slid slightly close to hers and he wrapped his arm around her. She leaned her head on his shoulder.

"Are you ready to eat?" Darrin asked.

"No, not yet. Let's just sit here for a little while longer. I really love this view, Darrin."

He took her hand and placed it against his face. She instinctively stroked his smooth skin. She wanted him to kiss her. And he read her mind. He moved his head, and touched his lips to hers. Wave after wave of searing passion moved over Deb's entire body, goose bumps rose hard and fast on her arms. She pulled him closer, his chest met hers. She began to rake her hands through his curly head of hair, then down his face and around his back. She stopped at the top of his behind.

She felt as if she were sinking as they descended into the mountain of pillows, his body pressed hard against hers. First their lips, then their tongues met, his fingers entwined in her hair. He broke their kiss only to move his lips lightly across her face, down her neck, then back to her lips. He left a trail of fire with each kiss. Deb moaned deep within the depths of her body. He intensified his kisses, his full lips upon a sensitive area between her neck and breasts. He stopped.

"I have waited for someone like you for so long," he whispered as their lips met over and over, again and again. She was lost in his touch, his embrace, as he quietly moved his body over hers, the feel of his full weight against her. They shuddered as his hands began a game of exploration, touching every inch of her. She closed her eyes and envisioned his hands moving across the tops of her breasts, down her stomach, onto her thighs, and then back up the same path to her face. He settled his body by her side and slowly began to unbutton her blouse, revealing her soft brown skin, heated from his touch. He raised himself slightly to look at her, a fierce fire in his eyes as he moved over her once again.

She tried to gain control of her senses, but with every kiss she lost her resolve and began to let her hands wander freely across his body. They floated wantonly down his back to stroke his taut behind. Her touch caused him to tense and he let out a deep throaty moan.

She had had enough. He was wild with desire. She couldn't stand it any longer. She squirmed from under him and sat up. She unbuttoned the first three buttons of his shirt, exposing his broad hairy chest. She kissed him in the center of his chest, her tongue flicking cross the hairs before she licked the tips of his nipples.

Suddenly he stood. She could see his chest glistening where she had just kissed him. He extended his hand and slowly pulled her to her feet. In one fluid motion, Darrin picked her up and carried her into his bedroom, his lips fastened upon hers. He slowly set her down and then pulled her close as he walked them toward the large bed. He sat with her facing him and continued to remove her blouse, methodically undoing each button. His eyes watered as he pushed the silk garment across her shoulders. His hands were nimble as they caressed her bare flesh. He inhaled deeply. The sight of her half naked body, her breasts covered by a shear bra caused him to tremble.

"Are you sure about this, Deb? I want you, I won't lie, but I want you to want me, too."

She placed her fingers upon his lips, followed by a long, deep kiss. She reached around her back, and in one quick motion unfastened her bra. She let it join her blouse on the floor. The sudden coolness caused her to shiver. Darrin began to place kisses on her full bare breasts; he paused to lightly lick the dark area around her nipples. All of her reserve eased away as Darrin's tongue play intensified as he kneaded the hardened tips between his teeth and lips. She tossed her head back and moaned, her hands trembling slightly as she urged his head further onto her breasts.

The light from the moon illuminated their bodies as Darrin lay back on the bed, pulling Deb onto him. Their gazes met, locked, until a quick and sudden wave of passion overtook them both. She could no longer deny the messages her body was sending, the feelings he had awakened.

He finished undressing her, again slowly and methodically. First he removed her boots, taking time to rub the soles of her feet. Next, he unzipped her slacks. He pulled them down slowly. His hands massaged up and down her stocking-clad legs. Finally, he removed her stockings, followed by her lace panties. He stood. His dark eyes searched hers as she lay naked in front of him.

"I knew every inch of you would be beautiful," Darrin said, his voice barely audible as he began to take off his clothes.

She searched for a change in him, a sign that maybe this wasn't supposed to happen.

"I can love you, Deb, you know that," Darrin implored. He took his time. He began with his shirt. His massive chest heaved with each motion, and he ended with his pants.

She was pleased to see him clad in black boxers, his muscular legs stretching the fabric, as he stood there, seemingly unsure of his next move. Deb knelt on the bed, removed Darrin's boxers, and sat back on the heels of her feet. Her eyes roamed without shame up and down the entire length of his toned body. His hairy chest, covered in a mass of dark curls, was wide, with pectorals that tapered down to a flat muscular stomach leading to his waiting member.

"Darrin, please come to me," Deb uttered, as she lay back on the bed and held her arms out to him. He eased his body onto the bed and moved into her open arms. She kissed him slowly at first and then hungrily.

Darrin broke their kiss. "I want to love you all night, Deb. Will you let me?"

He eased from atop Deb and lay next to her. He rubbed his hands over her entire body, pausing only long enough to explore her hidden crevices where he placed wet, warm kisses. And each spot he kissed left a burning, aching sensation in her, heightened when his lips moved to her special spot. She gasped and arched her back. He didn't stop, instead he teased her, his tongue play carrying her to that first wave, one that left her wanting, needing more of him. And just when she thought that he had awakened every inch of her being, her inner soul, he began to awaken other spots and she groaned uncontrollably.

"Are you sure about this, Deb? I didn't mean for this to happen tonight, it's just..." his words came out in short spurts. She pulled him by his shoulders to lie fully on top of her. She placed fiery kisses on his face and neck.

"Darrin, I'm sure," she breathed.

For a long while they lay in each other's arms. His heart beat wildly as he tenderly entered her, finally giving in to his own unfulfilled need. Deb raised her hips to meet him, their bodies becoming entwined as they explored the depths of their passion. He tightened his embrace as he began to move against and then with Deb's own motions. Her body reacted involuntarily as she felt another wave threaten to take over, control her. The closer she got, the more brazen she became and grabbed his behind to pull him deeper into her. As they neared the wave, he began to call out her name. The wave enveloped them both and their motions became more intense with Darrin loving her. They held on to each other while the wave covered them, swept them out into darkness, and then calmed them.

"I could make love to you forever," Darrin whispered, cuddling Deb in his arms as they reveled in the afterglow of their passion, the moon shining on their bodies.

Chapter Fifteen

It seemed that everyone around Deb began to notice a change in her. At work, her co-workers commented that she seemed to walk lighter, smiled more, and even went out to lunch during deadline. Something she never did before she met Darrin. Even Pat had a comment for her.

"Ah, the look of love," he said.

She had to admit that being with Darrin had brought out the best in her. It made her see beauty in just about everything. And after every date, he left her wanting more, but he always held back, saying the best was yet to come. But out of them all, Shari noticed the change and liked what she saw in her best friend.

"Deb is never home. And when she is, she is either on the phone with Darrin or getting dressed to go out with Darrin," Shari told Denise over the phone.

"Girl, she knows she is in love with that man. I don't know why she's still trying to fight it. And she even missed my annual Halloween Party. She's never missed that, even when she was dating what's-his-name," Denise said.

"Oh, I forgot, we are forbidden to say Mario's name. You know he's been calling again? He's

called damn near every day this week! Thank God
Deb wasn't here when he did." Shari cringed at the
thought of Mario trying to slither back into Deb's
life. "I think Mario realizes that Deb has found
somebody; now he's back trying to put a monkey
wrench in it."

"That's no good, Shari."

"Tell me about it," Shari responded, anger rising
in her voice. "But let me tell you Denise, as long as
I'm around, Mario won't be. You can put money on
that!"

"You got that right, Shari. But, you know how
Deb feels about us interfering in her affairs. She'd
kill us if we did!"

"Then I suggest you pick out your best Sunday
suit, cause we going to get murdered. If Mario so
much as shows his face on the corner three blocks
up, I'm gonna kill him. But, Denise, for real, we're
gonna have to sit close to this one. You know Mario
is one smooth-talkin' brother. And for once Deb is
really happy."

"What do you suggest?"

"I'm not sure right now, but let me think on it
and I'll let you know later."

☻ ☻ ☻

Deb held on to Darrin's arm as they walked out of
the lobby of the old movie theater. They had decid-

ed to go to a special screening of *Black Orpheus* at
the refurbished old theater which was once an
opera house. Darrin knew it was one of her favorite
movies.

Finally, her doubts had ebbed away, and she felt
safe, secure, in love. She wanted to kick herself for
all the tests she'd put him through, but she wanted to be sure this was real. She had to be sure that
he wasn't toying with her emotions. She knew she
couldn't live through another relationship like the
one she had with Mario.

She noticed the tall, leggy woman approach
them before Darrin did. The woman's eyes were
narrow as she got closer to them. Her flawless
mocha skin, and her hour-glass shape dressed in a
fashionable winter-white fitted, double-breasted
suit was impeccable. And the long Sable coat
thrown carelessly over her arm caused Deb to
wince at the mousy outfit she wore. But it was
something in this woman's eyes that made Deb's
hands sweat and her heart begin to pound in her
chest.

"Well, nice to see you again, Darrin. How have
you been?" the woman drawled evenly.

"Fine," Darrin responded. Deb could feel his
back stiffen. He stepped back an inch. "Um, Traci,
this is Deborah. Deborah, this is Traci."

"Hi," Traci responded. She tossed her head back
and waved a hand at Deb.

"Darrin, dearest, why haven't you returned any of my calls? I've tried calling you at the office and at home and you never seem to be there. Is this the reason why you are suddenly unavailable?" Traci whined.

Deb could see the anger in Traci's hazel eyes. She peered at Deb, even rolled her eyes at her.

"I've been busy," Darrin responded. "Besides, we've worked out all the details we need to."

"Too busy to call me back? Excuse us, please." Traci grabbed Darrin by the arm.

Deb stood there as they walked away from her, Traci's gait confident as she pulled Darrin off to the side. Deb watched Traci as she waved her hand in the air over her head, and then pointed directly at her, Traci's mouth moving rapidly. Every so often Traci threw her head back, then glared at Deb, while Darrin stood stiffly, absently nodding his head now and then.

Suddenly Deb became self-conscious. She began to mentally berate herself for wearing tweed pants instead of wool, for wearing a cotton turtle neck instead of silk. She grew increasingly agitated at the scene between Traci and Darrin. She felt foolish as she stood there and watched the man she was supposed to be with being tongue-lashed by another woman. And to top it off, it was the woman whom Darrin's aunts said he once wanted to marry.

Traci glared angrily at Deb before she stalked
off. She could see from the expression on Darrin's
face that he was worn, his eyes were angry. He
walked back to Deb.

"So, that was the infamous Traci?"

"How did you know about her?"

"Your Aunts mentioned her at the Bears game,
remember? They said you two were in love and
were planning to get married."

"Were is the operative word."

"She's awfully pretty. Is she a model?"

"No. A lawyer."

"How long did the two of you date?"

"One day too many," Darrin answered. Deb
noted the sarcasm in his words.

"Why do you say it like that? She must have
meant something to you. You were going to marry
her. Why didn't you ever mention her?"

"Nothing to tell. Look do we have to talk about
her?"

"No, we don't. Anyway, the second half is about
to begin."

For the first time since they began to date, an
uncomfortable silence grew between them, and it
frightened Deb. Once back in the theater she
noticed the set of Darrin's jaw, his anger, as he
stared straight ahead. He never looked her way.
She knew it was the same anger she'd witnessed
directed at his aunts, and it caused her to wonder

what Traci could have possibly done to him to make his mood change so suddenly.

Her mind raced. She missed the whole second half of the movie as she thought of ways to broach the subject of Traci and where she fit in his life. As they left, Deb could see that Darrin's mood hadn't changed. He seemed sullen, different.

A light snow had begun to fall, adding to the piles of white and gray slush along the sidewalk. Deb stomped the snow from her boots, then swung her legs into the car. On the drive home, they didn't speak, and she became increasingly agitated at his silence. When they pulled into the driveway, Deb had had enough.

"What did this Traci do to you, Darrin? Ever since we ran into her, you have been quiet and withdrawn."

"I'm okay. Can we just drop the subject? Are you available tomorrow?" Darrin said, ignoring her question.

"No! We can't drop it! She obviously meant something to you. Crossed you, broke your heart, or something. Otherwise you wouldn't be so angry."

"It's not important for you to know."

"Why isn't it? You're always telling me to ask and not assume, and now you're leaving me to draw my own conclusions. And trust me, they're nothing nice."

"Look Deb, I'm not going to hurt you, and there's nothing to tell. We broke up a long time ago. That's all." A frightening anger welled in his dark eyes, but Deb refused to let it go. All she had ever asked of him was to be straight with her and he had assured her over and again that he would.

"Darrin, it's evident that you and Traci have some unfinished business, so I tell you what. You just forget about tomorrow and any other night. I don't want to be in the way, and I certainly don't want to be someone that you rebound to." Deb grabbed the door handle and got out of the car. She slammed the door shut and stomped up the path to the porch steps.

She heard the wheels of Darrin's car screech as he gunned the accelerator and backed out of the driveway. She stood on the porch until the car's tail lights disappeared into the night. A hot mixture of anger and sadness suddenly enveloped her. She sat down on the snow-covered steps. She didn't notice the cold air as it swirled snow around her. Tears began to fall freely. Only when they began to sting her hot cheeks did she decide to go inside.

She silently tiptoed into the house. She didn't want to explain the events of the evening to Shari. Rocket sensed her sadness, licked her hand, and followed her up the stairs to her room. She tossed her coat and purse on the floor and flung her body, face down, onto the bed.

How could he react to Traci that way and not explain? She let her thoughts run rampant until she came to one that made her shake: "Maybe he's still in love with her," she said aloud.

Her tears soaked the pillow as she replayed Darrin's words of how he wanted to be an open book to her, yet he had never talked about Traci or the type of relationship they shared. She sat upright. Anger replaced her sadness and she wiped her face on her sleeve.

"Well, I'll be damned if I'm going to stand idly by and watch him and Ms. Traci resume their relationship. I have too much at stake! Next time! There won't be a next time!"

Her head began to throb with the very thought of Darrin playing her for a fool. She trusted him. Believed in him, in his words of love. But he was just like all the others. He would lie to get what he wanted. Now, she was alone once again, and she was tired. Tired of letting her guard down, tired of being lied to.

She got in bed. Better she know now before they started to talk about marriage.

The tears started again.

The actual thought of Darrin being with Traci caused her to go numb. She closed her eyes and fell into a fitful sleep.

In her dreams Darrin's sullen face didn't leave
her mind. In one dream she saw him walk down
the street arm in arm with Traci. She called out his
name several times, but he didn't hear or see her.
Then she heard them laughing, with Darrin saying
to Traci that he loved her. Deb ran behind them
and tried to grab Darrin's arm several times, but
her hand just slipped through his body. And then
they disappeared.

◎ ◎ ◎

Darrin pulled into the large parking garage. He
rubbed his head. Normally, he would let the valet
park his car, but on this night he didn't want to see
anyone. He parked, then used the freight elevator
up to his apartment.

He was angry with himself. Damn! He had handled that like a real champ. Why did he have to run
into Traci, of all people?

On his floor, he stepped off the elevator and
walked slowly down the dimly lit hallway. Damn
that woman! Traci had almost ruined him, and she
had the audacity to pretend as if nothing ever happened. And Deb—he couldn't bear to think of Deb,
and how hurt she must feel. All she wanted was for
him to be honest, and he had failed her.

He fumbled with his keys. He finally got into the
condo and went straight to his bedroom. Bright

moonlight spilled through the window. A moon two lovers should share. Instead, he had left Deb angry and unhappy. He knew he was wrong, knew he had hurt her. He had seen the pain he left behind, that same pain Mario had inflicted. He had promised not to ever hurt her. All he did was let her down. And for what. His ego. Why didn't he just come out and tell Deb all about Traci and how she made a fool out of him.

Pride had kept him silent.

Chapter Sixteen

For three weeks straight, Deb refused to take Darrin's phone calls. In the beginning she would just hang up on him and when that didn't work, she just stopped answering the phone altogether, letting the answering machine screen her calls. If he called her at work, she told the receptionist to say she wasn't available.

Shari began to worry. The light that she had seen in Deb's eyes had gone completely out. It was replaced by a vacant darkness that she didn't like to see at all. She knew that she had to figure out a way to get them back together—Deb deserved happiness. After all she'd been through, her mom dying, her brother moving, and that worthless Mario. And Shari knew that Darrin was just the one to make Deb happy. Shari called Denise.

"Won't you at least tell her that Traci and Darrin have been over for nearly two years," an exasperated Denise said.

"I've tried a thousand times, Ne, but she won't listen to me. Hell, I can't even mention his name."

"Gosh, that chick is stubborn. So, now what are we gonna do. We can't just leave things the way they are. Has Mario called?"

"Yeah. And I'm afraid that when Deb starts answering the phone again he's going to slither his way back."

"Then, Shari, we have no option but to interfere."

"What happened to your fear of the wrath of Deb?"

"I lost it after talking to Darrin yesterday. He admitted that he should have explained things when Deb first asked him, but he said the way this Miss-Traci-Thang dogged him caused him to react irrationally. He said something about having foolish pride. But now he has given up and is mad at Deb for the way she's been acting."

"Yeah, hanging up on him and refusing to take his calls. I swear." Shari rolled her eyes.

"Do you remember when he broke their first date?"

"Yeah, I remember. What about it?"

"Seems as if Miss Traci was the one behind the attempted take over of Darrin's company."

"Where did you hear that from?"

"Not from Darrin. Darrin's secretary, Sofia, told my friend Jon's secretary that Traci tried to ruin him by calling up all the shareholders. She told them that his new venture was riddled with mistakes and that if they didn't pull out now they would lose thousands of dollars. Now ain't that a kick in the teeth for ya?"

"I'll say."

"Darrin had to scramble like mad to convince the investors to believe in the new venture, something about going global."

"That would make me mad enough to want to kill," Shari answered. "But why would she do something like that?"

"Seems as if Ms. Thang got wind of Darrin's hot and heavy dating of Deb. And that's not all."

"Oh, God. There's more?"

"I'm afraid so," Denise replied. "Traci and Mario used to date."

"What? You're joking? When?"

"When he was dating Deb. Seems as if that hoochie at the club wasn't all Mario was into. Talk about small world."

"But the way Deb described her, Mario ain't her type."

"Now, we know Mario. He probably fed her some line and she fell for it. But here's the real kicker. Mario called this Traci chick and told her all about Deb and Darrin."

"How did he find out?"

"He and Jon are cousins."

"And you've been talking. Haven't you?" Shari sighed.

"I didn't see any harm. Anyway, that's water under the bridge. Now that we know the real deal behind all of this, what are we going to do?" Denise asked.

Shari's mind worked overtime as she tried to come up with plan after plan. Her eyes lit up.

"Wait. I've got an idea. Deb is going out of town to a conference tomorrow. Give me Darrin's office number."

"I thought you had it?"

"I don't have time to look for it. Just give it to me."

She closed her eyes and said a silent prayer. She felt she had no other choice but to interfere. She couldn't stand another day of watching her friend become more and more withdrawn.

"What are you going to do, Shari?"

"Ne, I don't have time to tell you. I'll call you back. Keep your fingers crossed. Bye." She hung up, then dialed the number Denise gave her.

"God, I hope this works, I really hope this works," she said aloud to herself.

"Wilson & Associates. May I help you?"

"Yes, would you please connect me to Mr. Wilson's secretary, Sofia."

"One moment please."

The phone went silent as Shari sat there and stared out her bedroom window, grateful that Deb was working late.

"This is Sofia, may I help you?"

"Yes, I sure hope you can. This is Shari Thomas and I'm a friend of Darrin's and Deborah."

"Ah, yes, Ms. Anderson. How is she?"

"Probably the same as Darrin." Shari chuckled nervously.

"I know. It's a shame. Mr. Wilson has been moping around here for weeks. Poor boy, I think he really liked Ms. Anderson," Sofia responded.

"Well, I have a plan, will you help me?"

◉ ◉ ◉

O'Hare Airport was crowded with scores of people. Deb frowned as she walked through the United terminal. She wasn't big on crowds. But she liked the terminal, the way the neon lights flicked red, and then blue. The lights were in sync with odd chimes which sounded more like the music from the movie *Close Encounters*. She rode the motorized treadmill, her face void of emotion as she thought about Darrin for what seemed to her the millionth time that day.

She was relieved to be going to Costa Mesa for a week. Even though it was a journalism conference for the job, she still felt that the time away and a little sun would do her some good.

"Ma'am, your ticket please," the deep voice of the flight attendant said to Deb. She handed him the ticket and boarded the plane, settling into her seat in first class, three rows from the cockpit. She kicked her small bag under the seat in front of her and laid her briefcase in the seat next to her. She hoped no one would be sitting next to her.

"Wait, Janice, don't close the door. We have another passenger. He's at the gate now," Deb overheard one attendant say to the other. She kept her head down, hoping whoever walked on the plane would pass on by and not try to sit beside her.

"Excuse me, is this seat taken?" a voice above her said.

No such luck. Deb looked up—straight at Darrin. "What the hell are you doing on this plane?" she demanded. Deb's astonished tone made several people turn to look at her.

"Deb, this is a free country and I can fly anywhere I choose to." Darrin barked. "And since I'm on this flight, apparently sitting next to you, you might as well get used to it."

She could see that he was just as stunned as she was. She contorted her face, pulled her small bag from under the forward seat and dropped it on top of her brief case. She then folded her arms across her chest.

"Look Deb, it's a long flight and I've got a lot of work to catch up on. So, now if you don't mind?" He snatched her bags out of the seat and dropped them in her lap. He glanced at her, shook his head and placed his bag in the overhead compartment.

Though she didn't want to, she watched his fluid movements, the strong arms that once held her. Her eyes threatened to water, but she forced back the tears.

They looked angrily at each other. She rolled her eyes at him and he sucked his teeth in response. He pulled a newspaper out of his brief-case, snapped it open loudly, and held the paper up to his face.

⊙ ⊙ ⊙

Of all the flights leaving for Costa Mesa, Sofia would book him on one with Deb on it. This had to be more than a coincidence. He hadn't seen Deb in over a month. His calls had gone unanswered, and he had finally given up. She just wouldn't give him the chance to make it up to her. He glanced at her, her warm beautiful face, and once again remem-bered the pain.

He had longed to hear her voice, hold her in his arms, kiss her, make love to her. But here she was acting like a spoiled child. He snapped the paper again.

"Sir, we are about to take off, please fasten your seat belt," the attendant said to him.

Darrin smiled warmly and complied, then glanced over into Deb's lap. "I suggest you do the same thing," he said flatly.

He watched as she snatched at her seat belt, jerking at the end. She pulled at it until it snapped her hand. A welt appeared instantly. He reached out to her. She pulled her hand back and tossed him an angry sideways glare.

"Fine, suit yourself." Darrin turned his attention back to his newspaper.

The words on the pages were unrecognizable. He couldn't concentrate. He started to speak to her, make her hear him out, but she placed her headsets over her ears, and turned up the volume. He looked squarely at her and snapped his paper again with a "humph."

❂ ❂ ❂

Throughout the five-hour flight, Deb and Darrin continued to exchange angry glances. When the flight landed, she climbed over him before he could unfasten his seat belt.

Outside LAX airport, Deb boarded the shuttle. Darrin followed.

"Damn. Why don't he go away?"

"Ma'am? You say something?" the driver asked Deb as he watched her through the rear-view mirror. She asked the driver to pull off.

"Ma'am, I must wait here another fifteen minutes until my scheduled departure time. Other people have paid for this shuttle."

She watched as Darrin ignored her and began a conversation with the driver.

Once the shuttle left the airport, the picturesque view of the ocean rolled by and softened Deb's agitation. Water normally calmed her but since her break up with Darrin, she hadn't wanted to walk along Lake Michigan. She twisted around in her seat and nodded off.

❊ ❊ ❊

"Costa Mesa is just around the bend here, it will take us just a few more minutes to arrive at the hotel," the driver announced.

The brightness of the sun shining through the van windows caused Deb to squint. She pulled out her sunglasses.

"I am lucky today," began the driver. "You both are staying at the same hotel."

An angry groan escaped Deb. Darrin glared at her. She glared back.

"I think there is some mistake. My reservations are at the Villa Costa Mesa," Darrin informed the driver.

"Sir, I am going to the Villa Costa Mesa, but it is actually the Hilton Villa Costa Mesa and her reservations are at the same place." The driver looked at both Deb and Darrin. "But, sir, if you are not pleased with your reservations, then you can try to change them."

"Try?"

"Yes, there are two conferences in town this week and both hotels are booked solid,"

"No, that's okay. She won't get in my way."

"Excuse me, sir?"

"Never mind."

Deb pretended not to hear his last words and turned her attention to the tall palm trees that lined the street. She noticed the mud-colored bricks of the hotel were covered by a lush grape vine, with green, yellow, and red speckled plants at the base.

"Welcome to the Villa, I mean, the Hilton Villa Costa Mesa. Please enjoy your stay," the driver announced as he climbed out of the van and ran to retrieve Deb's and Darrin's suitcases.

Deb climbed out of the back of the van and brushed past Darrin. He sighed. "What's the rush?"

She snatched her bag from the driver's hand and walked quickly into the hotel. She marched straight to the reservation desk, checked in, and headed for the elevator. As she waited she could hear Darrin's voice as he began arguing with the clerk.

"What do you mean that my room isn't available? What am I suppose to do? I have a dinner appointment with a client in an hour!"

"Mr. Wilson, we apologize for the mix-up, if you would give us just a few moments, we will have the situation rectified."

Deb smiled slyly.

"That serves him right. Always thinking he can get his way," she said loudly. She didn't care if he heard her or not. She pressed the elevator button again and hummed a tune, trying to recall the words to a song she overhead on the radio. She half sang, half mumbled the words to Vanessa L. Williams's song. When the elevator door opened, Deb had begun to sing loudly, "I won't come runnin' back..."

"I won't come runnin', runnin' back to you. No, I won't come runnin,'" Deb smiled.

The elevator carried Deb up to the 17th floor where her room was to be for the next five days. She walked gingerly down the hall, her gym shoes making a squeaking sound on the highly glossed tile floor. Her eyes glanced from right to left as she searched for her room number on the pale cream doors.

She placed the key card in the lock. When the door opened, her mouth opened wide and she let out a loud "wow" as she stepped into the room.

The room was large and impressive. She looked around, realizing that her room was a two-bedroom suite.

"Man, *Neighborhood Mag* sure knows how to spoil a person!" Deb laughed. She plopped down on an oversized peach-colored couch. She grabbed a pillow and tossed it in the air, glad to be away from Chicago and its harsh winter.

Touring the suite, she opened the mini refrigerator, looked at the assortment of expensive juices, nuts, beer, and wine. She decided on a can of fruit juice. Deb sipped the juice and headed to the large screen TV with a VCR built in sitting in an armoire. She searched for the remote, then turned on the television. In the middle of channel surfing, she noticed a small stereo, complete with a CD and a cassette deck in the corner opposite the wet bar. Deb got her pouch, pulled out a couple of CD's. She popped the disc of Yanni into the player, turned up the volume and continued to open doors.

Peach walls and mint-green carpet showed off the cream bed spread as Deb entered one of the bedrooms and sat down on the edge of the bed. On her left, the bathroom door was slightly open. Curious, she pushed it fully open and switched on the light.

The gold and white bathroom was larger than any she had ever seen. A shower stall was at the end of an enormous Jacuzzi. She ran and grabbed her suitcase, tossed it on the bed and rummaged through it. She retrieved the bath oil and the scented candles she had packed, then set them on the large vanity.

"A warm shower would be nice right about now. I'll save the bath for later," Deb said to herself. The string section of Yanni's "In My Lifetime" began to soothe her. She needed it after that nerve-racking encounter with Darrin. What rotten luck that she and Darrin had to be on the same flight, and now in the same hotel.

Deb unpacked, placed her clothes in the closet, and arranged toiletries on the vanity. She finished by taking the promised shower. And since the conference didn't begin until the next day, she was glad she had the whole evening to relax.

At least the conference would keep her busy enough. The chance of running into Darrin was slim to none. And to Deb, as the old saying went, slim just left. So, she was pleased that there would be little contact, if any, with him.

Deb decided to sit on the terrace. She wrapped her arms about her and basked in the cool breeze as the sun set. She laid her head back on the cushion of the overstuffed chair and closed her eyes. For the first time in weeks she didn't have Darrin's face floating around in her mind or want the feel of his body next to hers. She hoped that inner peace would come to stay.

"Anyone here?" a familiar voice called out.

She jumped up from the lounging chair, pulled her robe tightly around her and stepped into the living room.

"What are you doing here?" she asked. She couldn't believe he was standing right there in the middle of the living room. "How did you get in here?" she demanded.

"I should be asking you the same thing." Darrin eyed her. "The front desk assigned me this room. So, I suggest you get your things and find someplace else to sleep."

"Oh, no, my brother, I don't think so." Deb gripped the top of her robe. "Oh, we must fix this. As the saying goes: You ain't got to go home, but you got to get the hell out of here!"

"I think you mean, you've got to get out of here. I'm not going anywhere." Darrin dropped his bags on the floor and sat down on the sofa. Deb could see he was serious. And when he placed his feet on the coffee table and folded his arms across his chest, she knew it would take a bulldozer to move him.

She walked over to him, pushed his feet off the coffee table, then stomped over to the telephone.

"Front desk? I want to report a mistake. This is Deborah Anderson in room 1720. A Mr. Darrin Wilson is here, saying that this room belongs to him."

Deb tapped her foot while she listened to the desk attendant. She couldn't believe what she was hearing.

"Yes, I see, yes... But... I see... I see. Thank you for your help." She hung up the phone.

"What's the deal?" he asked without looking at her.

"It seems as if the room was booked for both of us. There were some last minute changes in the reservations. And they are booked solid, so even if I wanted to change rooms, I couldn't."

"Well, this one has two bedrooms and I promise you, I won't come near you." He rose and headed to the room on his left.

"Not that one! That one is mine. You take that room over there." Deb pointed to the right.

"Fine. Whatever. Listen, my business dinner was canceled, and—"

"So?"

He sighed before speaking. "So, the meeting has been changed to early tomorrow morning and I need to get some sleep. So, keep it down, if you don't mind."

"Sure I mind. I was here first and I had planned on watching a movie. So, you're going to have to try to sleep with a little noise."

He spoke between clenched teeth. "At least can you keep the volume down."

"Sure, I'll try," she responded, a hint of sarcasm in her voice. She had no intentions of going near him, nor doing the things she wanted to just because of him. Deb stood and watched him pick up his bags. He was pained, she could see that, but what about her? Maybe she was acting irrational. They were both going to have to share the space for the rest of the week. She wasn't sure if she could handle seeing him morning and night, especially at night.

"This is going to be some week."

Deb slammed the door to her room.

❂ ❂ ❂

The clock read three a.m. when Deb heard footsteps outside her room. She had just fallen asleep an hour earlier after tossing and turning from the same nightmare about Darrin and Traci she had been having for weeks. She sat up and saw the light filtering in under the closed door. She could see the shadow of Darrin's feet as they paced back and forth, coming near, then moving away from her door. This went on for several minutes until she heard Darrin's door shut. She lay back in her bed and moaned softly as she rocked her body against the firm bed. She shut her eyes tightly and willed herself to sleep.

Chapter Seventeen

For three days Deb and Darrin tiptoed around each other as if shards of glass were scattered across the floor. Exchanging an occasional sideways glance, neither uttered a word the whole time.

Much to her surprise, Deb had became accustomed to his morning rituals. He got up at five a.m. to work out in the hotel's gym for an hour. After that he would return to shower and dress, then order breakfast for both of them, though he never once asked her what she wanted to eat. He just seemed to know.

Deb attended the writing seminars during the day and the social events in the evening. She chatted with a few of the women at the seminar, but one in particular, Lolita, seemed to be drawn to Deb. She sat next to her at every workshop and ate her meals with Deb. She couldn't seem to escape Lolita, and Lolita didn't seem to want to shut up. Deb was in no mood for idle gossip. Yet, Lolita chattered on about any and everything.

Lolita was a petite woman with shoulder-length hair dyed a brazen blonde and an hour-glass figure. And though Deb thought she had on way too much makeup for the warm, humid climate, she could see that Lolita was actually very pretty.

When they walked through the lobby, Deb would become self conscious, not of her own looks, but for Lolita and the various outfits she wore. The day they went into town to shop, Lolita was stuffed in a pair of short shorts and a tight red tank top. Deb was relieved she had chosen to wear white jeans and a white shirt.

"Girl, this seminar is boring," Lolita huffed loudly. "But today I found something—or I should say someone—that might just make this whole trip worthwhile."

Deb nodded absently and turned to see Darrin standing in the doorway. She quickly turned her head and boarded the van to take them shopping.

"Girl, that's him. That's my pick-me-up!" Lolita squealed. She flashed her white, even set of teeth. Deb thought they were too big for her mouth.

"Who? Him?"

"Yeah, the cutie standing in the doorway. Girl, I saw him in the lounge the other night and I about died. I sat next to him. He said very little. No matter how many questions I asked, he gave me one-word answers. But he's gonna fall. They all do."

"Oh, really?"

"Yup. But there was something awfully sad about him. He seemed lonely. And me being the sucker for sad eyes and a cute face, I tried my damnedest to cheer him up."

"What did you do?" Deb asked. She tried not to sound interested.

"Men are always suckers for the helpless routine. So, I made up this crap about my boyfriend cheating on me."

"What did he say?"

"He gave me some babble about the importance of trust and honesty, and some other armchair psycho babble. Girl, I wasn't interested in all that, I was too busy looking into those dark eyes. Damn, he had the sexiest pair of black eyes I've ever seen."

"Oh, yeah?" Deb grumbled. She remembered the last time she saw those black eyes, filled with pain the night they ran into Traci. She grimaced at the thought, as Lolita continued talking about Darrin.

"Now, gimme a man with eyes like that, and I'm all his."

"All whose?"

"Girl, you ain't listening. I'm still talking about the cutie in the doorway!"

"Well, did you get this cutie's name?"

"Yeah, he told me." Lolita waved her hand in the air, her cat-like nails decorated in three colors. "Derrick, David, D-something. But, I'll get it tonight."

"How do you know that?"

"Well, he's gotta eat sometime, and I plan to wait in the lounge. If not tonight, there's always tomorrow."

Deb winced at Lolita's referral to Darrin. As the van pulled away from the hotel, she could still see Darrin as he leaned against the wall, his arms folded across his chest. Though she couldn't see his eyes—they were covered by sunglasses—she knew the pain they held.

❂ ❂ ❂

Darrin watched Deb and the woman from the lounge. He fixed his stare on Deb. Damn! Why was this going so wrong? He had intended to speak to Deb when he spotted her in the lobby but changed his mind when he saw her with that obnoxious woman from the lounge. This wasn't as he planned. First the plane ride, which was literally a nightmare, then the room mix-up, followed by one appointment after another being canceled. He was going back to Chicago the next day and he knew that they would have to talk. He wanted to clear the air. He didn't want this hanging over his head.

After the van pulled away, he sat down in an armchair in the lobby. He rubbed his hands one over the other. Getting Deb to listen to him wasn't

going to be easy. But he owed her an explanation.
But more importantly, he knew he loved her.

Chapter Eighteen

Deb tossed the packages on her bed and flopped down beside them. When she rolled over, she noticed the note pinned to the bed spread.

"Deb, I'm leaving tomorrow morning," the note began. "Please meet me tonight at seven in the lounge. We need to talk. Darrin."

She crumpled up the note and threw it on the floor. She stared up at the ceiling. What could he possibly have to say? She had said all she was going to say to him, therefore there was no need to meet. Then she remembered Lolita. And even though Deb knew that on a good day, Lolita was not his type, this was a bad day for him and he might just be enticed by her.

It's none of my business, she told herself. She twirled her hair around her finger. But Lolita said he looked sad and lonely and she was going after him. That type of woman would hurt him even more. She would rather see Darrin with Traci than Lolita. It was something in the way Lolita talked about claiming and then discarding men that caused her to be concerned.

But Darrin was a grown man! He could take care of himself.

After Several hours of arguing back and forth,
Deb decided to meet him. What harm could come
from just talking to him?

○ ○ ○

The small tables in the dimly lit lounge were covered with white tablecloths. Candles burned in
short, tri-colored glasses. Deb stood at the
entrance. She spotted him at the bar, his back to
her. His head was bowed, his hands wrapped
around a glass. Sadness washed over her. The
closer she got, the more she wanted to reach out,
take him in her arms and love his hurt away. But
she was hurt, too. He had promised her to be open
and honest with her, that was all she asked of him,
yet when it came to her questions about his relationship with Traci, he chose to remain silent. As
Deb passed the last table that separated her from
Darrin, she heard Lolita's voice, low and seductive.

"Anyone sitting here?" Lolita purred as she
moved in on Darrin like a cat on the prowl.

"No," Darrin answered without looking up.

"Good. Lolita Matthews. What's your name
again? I'm sorry, I'm bad with names." Lolita stuck
out her cat-clawed hand.

"Darrin," he answered flatly.

"Well, Darrin, I'm sure your mama gave you a
last name."

"Wilson. Sorry, nice to see you again." He shook her hand.

"Sugar, you seem preoccupied. Maybe I can help this time," Lolita crooned.

Deb watched her place her hand on Darrin's forearm. She grew angrier by the moment as she witnessed Lolita's come-on.

Deb threw her shoulders back, lifted her head and resumed walking toward them.

"You know," Lolita purred, "if you talk about what's on your mind, it will get better. Take it from me, I know. Your advice the other night helped me immensely and to show you my gratitude, let me buy you a drink."

"That's okay, Lolita. Thanks, I've met my limit. Besides, I'm waiting for someone."

"Well, we can still have a drink until he gets here. Bartender, give me a Strawberry Daiquiri and give the gentleman here whatever he's drinking." Lolita waved nonchalantly at the man. She pulled Darrin by the arm and nestled her body close to his.

Deb had had enough of the show. It was time to break up this little happy tryst. She stopped on the opposite side of Darrin and glowered at Lolita.

"Hi, there," Darrin said when he saw Deb. He pulled out the empty bar stool next to him. "Thanks for meeting me."

"Well, well, Miss Lolita," Deb said, mocking Lolita's seductive tones. "I see you found him. Did you get his name?" Deb leaned over Darrin and smiled triumphantly when Lolita's expression changed.

"Why Deb, what are you doing here?" Lolita hissed, trying to retain her composure, but obviously failing.

"I'm meeting Darrin. He asked me to meet him here tonight."

"Oh, I see. Well, then we'll have a party. Bartender! Deb, what are you drinking?"

"I need something strong. Those trendy drinks just don't do it. I'll take a White Russian, Absolut vodka," Deb ordered and continued to stare at Lolita.

Darrin's head turned from Deb to Lolita and then back to Deb, a bemused look on his face as he sat between the two women.

"Lolita, didn't I hear you say that you were going to attend the early morning seminar? You know you need all the beauty sleep you can get, " said Deb.

"No," Lolita retorted. "As a matter of fact, I've decided not to go to the seminar. But, didn't I hear you say that you were expecting an important phone call?"

Darrin chuckled. Both women looked at him. His smile quickly faded.

"Darrin," Deb said and cleared her throat, "what is it you wanted to talk to me about?"

"Deb, I think the man is slightly busy right now." Lolita's eyes were enraged. "Besides, he's waiting for someone. Business. You understand. So, why don't you just go back to your room and wait for that phone call."

Deb smiled demurely, took her drink from the bartender, took a sip, got up and stood between Darrin and Lolita. She closed her eyes, counted to three, and then opened them again.

"Look, Lolita, didn't you hear him?" Deb pointed over her shoulder. "I'm the someone who has business to take care of with this man. You understand, don't you?"

"I haven't a clue what you're talking about," Lolita responded. She tried to push Deb aside. Deb's drink tipped and spilled down the front of Lolita's black spandex dress.

"Damn, Girl!" Lolita jumped off the bar stool, the drink dripping down the front of her. Her cat-like eyes became mere slits as she looked at Deb and then to Darrin.

"I'll be back, that you can count on!" Lolita said angrily and stormed out of the lounge.

"We'll be right here." Deb waved to Lolita's back.

"Well, I say!" Darrin said with a laugh. "Now, that was a cat fight! Meow!"

"That's not funny. She wouldn't go away." She sat on the stool Lolita had vacated.

Deb and Darrin continued to laugh. Some of the tension began to ease between them. Deb ordered another drink. She set the glass on the bar. The words she wanted to say to him weren't coming as easily as she had hoped. She cleared her throat.

He spoke first. "Deb, did you say something?"

"No," she replied in a low husky tone.

Their eyes wandered around the bar, the silence was unbearable. Both spoke at once.

"Deb?"

"Darrin?"

"You go ahead, Deb."

"No, Darrin, you first. You invited me here, remember?"

He nodded. "I know I should have explained about Traci, but she made such a fool of me that I just wanted to forget all about it. And when we ran into her, I got angry all over again. I know I should have told you the whole story, but I didn't, and I don't exactly know why." He paused.

Deb was silent.

"Anyway, I trusted her with my business, my emotions. And when I no longer trusted her with my emotions, I shouldn't have trusted her with my business. Of course, I didn't see her for the manipulative, spoiled brat she actually is."

"But, Darrin, your aunts said you were planning to get married. Is that true?"

"Yes, I'm afraid it is." He twirled the straw around in his glass. He continued to stall, glancing at his watch, then the bar, and then back to his drink, before he spoke again.

"How can I begin to explain this to you? Yeah, I thought I loved Traci. She is everything a man would want. She's smart, pretty, independent. But she's not everything I want or need."

"But I don't understand, Darrin. What's so hard about telling me that? I mean, I thought I really loved Mario until..."

"Until what, Deb?"

"Oh, never mind. The point is, that we have both been somebody's fool. The thing is not to be the same fool twice. Now, what's so hard about that?" Deb asked, her right hand placed firmly on her hip.

"Deb, a man is embarrassed when he lavishes a woman with expensive gifts and she plays him like a violin. I tried to buy Traci's love, when in fact I really didn't love her at all. I was just...I was just stupid! Happy that a woman like her would pay any attention to a man like me."

"Now, that's ego talking. You let your ego rule, and you got hurt. But so what, we've all been hurt. Listen to me, I've got nerve."

"Say, we better get out of here before Ms. Lo-li-ta comes back," Darrin offered. "And from the look on her face, she plans on coming back with a vengeance."

Without waiting for an answer from her, he stood up, tossed a few bills on the bar, took Deb by the elbow and escorted her out of the lounge.

"Where are we going?"

"The only place we can talk in peace. Our suite."

Her palms began to sweat as she tried to think of a better place for them to talk. And though she loved the look and feel of the suite, she knew it sent signals of arousal to her senses, causing her body to ache for Darrin's touch. She was aware of this the first time she stepped into the suite.

They stepped out of the elevator. Deb was forced to look at his back as he walked ahead of her to the room. He took his key card out of his pocket and for the first time that evening, she noticed that Darrin was wearing a pair of tan Dockers and a white short-sleeved polo shirt. His taut muscles strained at the sleeves of the fabric as he placed the key card in the lock.

"After you." He stepped to one side, his hand outstretched.

"Forever the gentleman," Deb said as she walked past him.

She sat on the couch, closest to the end. Darrin disappeared into his room. When he returned, he was dressed in shorts and a white T-shirt. Deb shuddered at the thought of him fully unclothed.

He sat at the other end of the couch.

"Deb, all I can say is that I am sorry and that I should have told you about Traci. I promised that I would never hurt you." He moved closer to her and she could see that he was serious. "I know you're angry with me. You have every right to be, but can you at least forgive me? Since you've stopped talking to me, I can't think straight. I can't even sleep in my own bed, because I keep thinking of you lying next to me." His words trailed off. Deb knew he wasn't sure if his words would affect her.

"Well, that's all I wanted to say to you, Deb. I just wanted to say that I'm sorry. I'm going to pack. My flight is at eight in the morning," He rose from the couch.

Deb's mind began to replay, like a video, all the times she had spent with him. Their walk on the pier after the Bear's game, the carriage ride when he kissed her, the way his body felt when he made love to her. Deep down she knew that who he was, what he was offering, was exactly what she had always wanted in her life. Still it seemed that the pain in her heart continually threatened to take over. She wrestled with her feelings and sat unmoving as Darrin headed for his room. No! She couldn't stand the thought of never seeing him again.

"Darrin, wait." Deb jumped up from the couch. "I owe you an apology, too."

"No, you don't. I probably would have reacted the same way. Maybe even worse. I just want you to forgive me. Will you? No. Can you forgive me?"

"Darrin, only if you forgive me. I should have at least given you the opportunity to explain. But I didn't. I overreacted."

"Deb, I could never really be mad at you. Even when you were rude to me on the plane, climbing over me. And then in the van..." Darrin laughed. She slapped him on the arm. They both laughed.

"It was silly, wasn't it?"

"I'll say. You even tried to kick me out of my own room!"

"Correction, my room!"

The ease they had once share with each other began to return. They sat close on the couch.

"Truce?"

"Truce," Deb responded and extended her hand to Darrin. He took it in his, lightly shook it, but didn't let go.

"Deb, I missed you. I missed your laughter, our laughing together, eating dinner with you, going to the show. Hell, I guess I just plain old missed everything about you."

"I sort of miss you too."

"Sort of? What do you mean, sort of? How could you not miss this dashing, debonair face." He turned his face to the side and scrunched up his nose.

She snickered at his expressions and rubbed his hand. "Okay, okay, I missed you."

"Good. Now, what are we going to do about it?"

"About what?"

"Deb, come on. You know what I mean. What are we going to do about us? I know I don't want to continue like this. I want you, Deb. I want you in my life, in my bed. I want to wake up and know that you are there." He became serious as he stared at her. "I'll wait forever if I have to."

"Darrin, I don't know. I don't know anything anymore." Deb walked to the patio window and pulled back the shades. The clouds had gathered angrily as they rolled and tumbled across the near blackened sky. She heard a clap of thunder in the distance followed by a streak of lightning that lit up the night sky. Her body stiffened when he came and stood behind her.

"How do you start over, Darrin? I don't know where to begin."

"We can start now, right here." He turned her to face him. He kissed her lightly on the lips. "Like this." His voice lowered and he placed another kiss on her lips, this time letting his cover hers. He pulled her into his arms.

All of her reservations began to melt away. That odd feeling in the pit of her stomach began to creep up and take over. She knew it, felt it, and was powerless to do anything but accept what she knew lay ahead. His kisses grew more and more intense. Her body reacted to the fiery message relayed. She caressed his face and hair and moaned loudly when the fire of his passion trailed down her body.

"I love you, Deb. Let me show you that I love you." He swept her up into his arms and carried her into the bedroom.

In one motion he pushed the clothes and packages to the floor and gently laid Deb down on the bed. Between each searing kiss he removed another article of her clothing until she lay bare before him, naked and vulnerable.

"Deb, I love you. Love me back."

He removed his own clothes. For a moment she wasn't sure. But when he touched her, lowering himself to enter her, she knew it was all real. The wave began its descent.

"Deb, do you love me?" Darrin breathed into her ear. "Tell me you love me. I know you do."

He continued to move inside of her, his thrusts becoming more concentrated. Her hips took over as she began to counter his thrusts. She captured his body, pulled him closer, and cried out as the wave surged over her entire body. But he wasn't finished with her and he moved forward, his motions more intense. She felt herself falling, reaching yet another wave.

She could contain the truth that welled up from within no longer. "Darrin, yes, yes, I love you. I've always loved you."

He slowed the rhythm, but Deb became wild as his strong body coupled with hers. She knew he was close to his own climax. She placed her legs around his waist and made their bodies one. He held her tight as the wave took over.

Outside, the rain fell. Drops made a rhythmic sound against the window.

"Deb, I won't make any promises this time, but I will try never to hurt you again," He stroked her hair as she laid her head on his chest.

The thunder became louder. Lightning lit up the room. They continued to hold each other and fell into a deep, peaceful sleep.

❁ ❁ ❁

The sound of a closing door caused Deb to jolt upright. She looked around the room, her eyes darting from the bathroom to the night stand. She leaned over the side of the bed, smiled, and lay back. Her and Darrin's clothing were carelessly strewn across the floor and it reminded her of the passionate love they made the night before.

Their scents, their colognes, their bodies, the aura of their love hung heavy in the air. Deb let out a loud sigh, pulled the covers over her naked breasts, and called forth her memory to re-live their fervent love making. Her heart raced and her body tingled as if he were still touching, kissing her.

"Deb? Are you awake?" Darrin called from outside the room. He smiled as he peeked around the partially opened door. She pulled the covers up around her shoulders.

He kicked the door open with his foot, a tray in his hands. She raised an eyebrow at his silk black boxers that clung seductively to him. He set the tray on the small table by the windows and began to arrange the plates, two napkins nearby, then ended it with a small glass vase with a single red rose in it.

"I take it you slept well? I know I did. I hope you're hungry. I ordered room service. I thought maybe we'd have breakfast inside today." He faced her. "Where's your robe?"

"It's—"

"Never mind. I've got something better in mind. I'll be right back." Darrin walked out of the room and returned with his pajama shirt. "Here. You can wear this."

His eyes grew dark. A poignant gaze appeared as he watched her allow the sheet to fall to her waist. The nipples of her full breasts reacted to the sudden chill in the air. She quickly put on his shirt and slid off the bed. Darrin's long shirt slid down her body. He wrapped his arms around her.

"I'm really glad we've made up, Deb. I missed you." He pulled her close, lifted her chin, and kissed her full on the lips.

She reveled in his kiss, the play of their tongues. Again her body reacted when his hand moved down her back and rested on her behind.

"Deb, I think we better eat before the food gets cold," Darrin moaned.

"Yeah, we should."

They got up and went to the table. Darrin sat across from her. She rubbed her stomach when it growled at the aroma of the food.

"I take it I made the right selection?"

"Yes you did. I love waffles. Thank you." Deb smiled. "What happened to your early flight?"

"I decided that what was here, lying next to me, was much better than sitting on a stuffy airplane all alone." He winked, a mischievous grin on his face.

"I see."

"You know, Deb, I enjoyed the way we made up last night." He took her hand in his. "I hope you plan to stick around awhile."

"Where am I going, Darrin? I mean, I want to be with you, but I just—"

"But, what? You don't know?" Darrin's eyebrows raised. "Look, I'm not afraid to love you. And yes, I was once like you, afraid to show my heart, to feel for anyone. But Deb, I have grown and so have my feelings for you."

"Your feelings for me?"

"Deb, let's be honest. I love you. You know this. I think I proved that over and again. Hell, Deb, I love everything about you."

Deb sat silent. An inexplicable swell of fear and confusion overcame her. She began to wonder, how could she accept Darrin's offer when she was so unsure about herself, her own feelings. She flinched as more thoughts filled her head. After all that had happened, was she ready? Could she be sure that she could love Darrin the way he wanted, needed to be loved? She was beginning to regret last night.

"Love? Darrin, you hardly know me. How can you love me?"

"How can you say I don't know you? I know you! I know your body, your heart, your soul. Damn, how much more do I have to know?" His eyebrows met in a scowl.

"Darrin, it's just that I've been hurt before, and by you. And to be honest, I'm not looking to be hurt again."

"Oh, and now I don't know a damn thing about a broken heart?" he replied. "Deb, how long will you continue to let your past chase you from your future? I can love you if you only give me—give us—

a chance. I know I messed up, but I thought we resolved that."

"We did...I mean, we have. But things have gone a bit faster than I was ready for."

"So, what are you trying to say? That it was a mistake for us to make love last night? It was a mistake for us to be here? What?"

"All I'm trying to say is that I'm not sure if I'm ready to handle what you're offering. That's all."

Darrin threw his napkin to the floor and walked to the bedroom door. "You know, Deb, you will let the ghost of Mario, and anyone else that makes one mistake, keep you from loving again. And that's a damn shame. So, how about you call me when you've decided to kill that ghost." He took another step toward the door. He placed his hands over the door frame and sighed loudly. When he turned, Deb could see the pain in his face and in his eyes. "And trust me, I won't wait for long. I have feelings, too. Contrary to popular belief, men do love—all of us aren't Mario!" He walked out and slammed the door behind him.

She was startled by the anger in Darrin's voice. She had spoken how she felt, or had she? Maybe her feelings for Darrin were deeper than she allowed herself to feel. A deep sadness engulfed her as she played with the petals of the single red rose. She heard the phone ring in the living room.

"Hold on," she heard Darrin say. "Deb! Telephone!" he yelled.

She walked out into the living room and caught a glimpse of Darrin's back as he walked into his room. The door slammed behind him.

Deb picked up the phone. "Hello?"

"Deb? It's me, Shari."

"Hi, what's wrong?"

"I think I should be asking you that. What's going on? Darrin sounded angry."

"How did you know that it was Darrin?"

"I didn't. I mean, I know his voice."

"Oh. Why are you calling?"

"Checking up on you. Back to Darrin. I didn't know he was going to California."

"Yeah, he and I were on the same flight, sat next to each other, rode the same van here, and even ended up sharing the same suite."

"So, have you all made up or should I take a cue from Darrin's voice? What's going on, Deb?"

"Shari, it's long and complicated, and I'm already late for a seminar. I'll tell you when I return. Bye!" She hung up before Shari could respond.

Chapter Nineteen

Deb rode in silence to LAX. A single tear rolled down her cheek as her mind traced back to the day before when Darrin left her and Costa Mesa altogether. She attended the rest of the seminars, unable to concentrate on any of the information the facilitators gave. She even had no energy to square off with Lolita and was able only to muster a weak sideways glance when Lolita strolled by her in the hotel lobby.

Darrin's pain-laden eyes remained etched in her mind, his words fast and angry before he walked out of the suite. "Deb, I love you, I won't lie and I want you in my life, but I'm not going to wait forever."

Deb winced as she recalled the sound of the slamming door. And she had cried when he left.

What have I done? she asked herself over and over as she absently showered and dressed for the seminar that day. When she looked in the mirror, her tear-swollen eyes had stared blankly back.

Deb continued to look out the van's window, the overcast sky making her feel even more sullen. She tried to lay her head back, close her eyes, but every time she did she saw the hurt in Darrin's eyes.

"Ma'am, we will be arriving at LAX in about a half hour. An hour if traffic is bad."

Deb nodded listlessly. A concerned look spread over the driver's face.

"You know, Ma'am, if you talk about what hurts you, you will feel better. I could even be of some help."

"No, not this time. I've really messed things up."

"Nothing's ever as bad as it seems. Give it a try."

Deb looked at the driver's reflection in the rear view mirror. His smooth olive skin didn't match the years of wisdom in his light-brown eyes. She shrugged and began telling him the whole story, even the part about how Darrin left.

"Ma'am, men can only be rejected so many times," the driver said in his slight Italian accent. "We are taught that emotion is a bad thing, no? And when we fall in love—amour—we fall hard. This, what did you say his name was?"

"Darrin."

"This Darrin wants love. And it seems as if he wants it from you. Now, this, forgive me, I'm bad with names. What was the last boyfriend's name?"

"Mario," Deb answered flatly.

"Ah, yes, Mario. Now, Mario is afraid of what love could do for him. And he hurt you bad, this I can tell, but this Mario is not the one for you. You want love, no?"

"Well, I guess I do."

"Come on. We all want to be loved. Why not let Darrin love you?"

"I'm afraid," Deb admitted. She looked away from the driver's face in the rear view mirror.

"Now, see? You've admitted it. Now you are ready to move forward. This love you want will come now. Just watch and see. And when you get back to Chicago, call Darrin and apologize. I bet you he take you back like this." The driver snapped his fingers.

"I don't know."

"I tell you what I do know. Love is never easy, but it is wonderful just the same. All you ask, all anyone asks, is to be loved. Let him love you."

Deb looked out the window at the sun peeking through the dense clouds. She let the driver's words sink in.

Her mood picked up. She had made up her mind.

❂ ❂ ❂

Deb paid the cab driver, stepped out of the cab, then strolled up the walk to her front porch.

In the living room, she sat on the couch where she and Darrin used to sit.

"He was offering me the world, and I couldn't accept it," she said to Rocket and smiled when the dog jumped up and placed her paws on her hands. "I missed you too, girl." She rubbed the top of

Rocket's head, then picked up the mail from the table and headed to her room. The message indicator on the answering machine blinked furiously. She said a silent prayer as she pushed the button and sat down on her bed. She absently flipped through the mail, her mind fully focused on the voices coming from the answering machine.

Message after message came from people she didn't care to hear from. But no message from Darrin. She felt dejected. She needed to run, something she hadn't done in months. She searched for her sweat suit. Deb was on the floor looking under her bed for her shoes when her heart stopped cold at yet another unwanted message. The voice, shallow and hard, leaked out of the machine.

"Hi, Deb. You know who this is. I've been calling you for weeks, you must be awfully busy. So, if you get this message give me a call. I miss you, baby."

Deb shivered at the familiar voice, its deepness. She sat on the floor. It had been a long time since she had last spoken to Mario, and then she had been rude to him. What could he possibly want?

She opened the drawer of her nightstand and fished out her old phone book with Mario's number in it. She dialed. The answering machine picked up and played Mario's patented message: "Hey, this is you know who and I'm you know where, so leave the you know what." Beep

Deb hung up. She cursed herself for even dialing the number. She went back to searching for her other shoe when the phone rang.

"Hello?"

"Hey baby, why'd you hang up?"

"Mario?"

"It's me, baby. How you doin'?" Mario spoke seductively.

"I'm fine."

"Say, I know how you look. I asked how you're doin'."

"Mario, that's tired. Haven't you come up with anything original yet?"

"You used to like that one, Deb. Once upon a time it made you smile."

"That was when I didn't know any better. What's up?"

"Nothing. Where have you been? I've called you just about every night for a month and you're never home. You must have a boyfriend? I know you got a boyfriend."

"And so what if I do?"

"Is he treating you right?"

"Now, Mario, come on. I know you didn't call to ask about my love life."

"What if I did? Then what? I might just want to know."

"For what?"

"Deb, I miss you. I really do. Life ain't been the same since we broke up. Look, I know I was a cad."

"Hell, that's putting it mildly!"

"Let me finish. Anyway, I know I hurt you, but I want to make it up to you. If you give me one last chance, I promise you I will never hurt you again."

"Now, where have I heard that one before? Mario, your chances of making it up to me are slim to none. And guess what?"

"I know, I know, slim just left. But for real, Deb, I've changed. You changed me. Let me prove it to you. Go out with me tomorrow night. Dinner, maybe even a show. Let me show you how much I've changed."

Deb listened to him. She admitted she was curious. Besides she had really messed things up with Darrin, and he probably was finished with her. She knew she had missed out on the opportunity to be with Darrin.

"Why not? What can a little date hurt."

"So, the answer is yes?" Mario asked. "You won't regret it. I promise you, you won't. I'll call you tomorrow."

Deb hung up the phone. She couldn't believe she just agreed to have dinner with Mario, of all people. She grabbed the phone and called Mario back, but his answering machine picked up again.

"Mario, call me when you get a chance. You've got the number. I've...never mind." She hung up.

What have I gotten myself into this time? Deb sighed, pulled on her running shoes, and grabbed Rocket's leash.

❈ ❈ ❈

Shari was on the couch, her arms folded across her chest, when Deb walked into the house.

"So, you've given up on Darrin?" Shari jumped to her feet and faced Deb. "Damn, Deb, when are you going to stop letting Mario get in the way of your happiness? I went through all that trouble for you and Darrin to end up apart anyway!"

"What trouble? Shari, what are you talking about?" Deb eyed Shari. She removed Rocket from the leash. "Just exactly what did you do?"

"I might as well tell you. I'm sure by now Darrin has fired his secretary."

Deb sat on the couch. Shari told her the story of how she and Darrin's secretary arranged for them to be on the same flight, in the same van, and in the same room.

"Darrin was sent down there on some phony business," Shari ended.

"Some phony what? You mean to tell me the whole thing was staged?" Deb shouted.

"Look, Deb, you're stubborn and a bit foolish if you ask me."

"Well, I'm not asking you. But, Shari, I do recall asking you to stay out of this! To let me handle it. And you gave me your word that you would!"

"But Deb, I saw how unhappy you were without Darrin. I just had to do something. So, that's what I did. Please don't be mad," Shari pleaded.

"Mad? I'm furious. How could you, Shari? I can handle things on my own."

"I can see that. You can really handle things," Shari responded sarcastically. "You handled Darrin so well that you've chased him away. And for what? Mario? You know, now that I think about it, I don't care if you are mad. But you should be mad at yourself for being so damn stupid. Who do you think you're fooling?"

"That's it, Shari. You've gone too far on this one," Deb shouted back. She ran upstairs, slammed the door, and sat in her window. She was enraged. First at Shari for not keeping her word, then at herself for being so stupid to agree to meet Mario. But more than anything she was angry at herself for carrying around the baggage of her failed relationship with Mario.

A tear rolled down her cheek. She held her head in her hands and admitted to herself that Shari was right.

She lay down on her bed and blinked at the ceiling. Her mind was crowded with thoughts of Darrin's body close to hers, Shari's condemnation of her actions, and Mario's words of apology. She was more confused than ever. She began to think of Mario, his smooth voice and smooth words.

She pulled a pillow over her face and began to yell. "What have I done? I made a date with Mario!"

Deb had made the date, and though she had no intentions of letting it go any further than just dinner, she knew her curiosity about Mario was getting the best of her.

There was no harm in going out with him one time. What would it hurt? Deb asked herself. Her mind told her, "Plenty!"

◉ ◉ ◉

Deb dressed quickly. She topped off her black jeans, black turtle neck, and a red blazer with a pair of snake-skinned black boots. Shari would kill her if she knew that she was going to meet with Mario tonight. Deb tipped down the stairs. She wanted to meet Mario outside. Just as she quietly shut the door behind her loud music could be heard down the block. She knew it was Mario. As the car approached the house, MC Hammer's "Can't Touch This" blared and vibrated the windows. The music was intrusive, and she knew for sure that her neighbors would be looking out their windows because of the disturbance.

"Say there beautiful." Mario screamed over the music as Deb got in the car.

"Can you turn that down? Better yet, either change it or turn it off completely." Deb shouted back.

"Sure, baby. Whatever you want is fine by me." Mario leaned over, turned off the radio, and kissed Deb on the cheek.

She reeled back. "Now, let's get one thing straight, this is just dinner. This is not a date."

"You're saying that now, but you won't be for long. You'll be singing my praises. You'll see."

Deb sighed and rolled her eyes as he pulled away from the curb.

All evening Deb sat across from Mario at the small Mexican restaurant and listened to him go on and on about himself and all the things he was doing. She nodded and responded to his self-praises in monosyllables. Finally, when she could take it no longer, she asked to go home.

"We were just gelling. You gotta go so soon?" Mario asked.

"I've got a lot of work to do. I just got back in town, so I'm loaded with stuff to do for Monday. You understand, don't you?"

"Yeah," he said. "Maybe we can do this again. I've enjoyed seeing you. You're really looking good, Deb, you know that?"

That all too familiar look crossed his face when his eyes roamed over her breasts. She frowned at him when he salaciously licked his lips just as she stood. She pulled her coat tightly around her.

"You know we can go back to my place."

"No, I've really got to be getting on home."

"Are you going to work tonight?" Mario asked her.

"Look, Mario," she snapped. "Just take me home, okay?"

"Yeah, yeah, you don't have to get funky on me, now. I was just askin'. Come on."

As they neared the exit, a small woman stepped in front of them. Deb had seen the woman somewhere before.

"So, here you are!" the woman shouted. "And who the hell is this?"

Both Deb and Mario stepped backward, and the woman moved in closer to Mario. She began to flail her arms, her curse words loud and unending. People in the restaurant turned and stared.

"You so full of shit, Mario, you stink," the woman screeched. "But, you ain't gonna get away that easy! Think you all that! Well, I say you ain't! You hear me? You ain't!"

"Aww, now Nita, I ain't doin' nothin' but havin' an innocent dinner. She invited me out!" Mario pointed to Deb.

Deb's eyes widened. She couldn't believe he
would tell such a lie. Then again, it was perfectly
believable: It was Mario. And if her memory served
her right, the one thing he did do well was lie.

She dismissed him and the woman with a wave
of her hand and continued out of the restaurant.
She turned to look at the woman again and realized
it was the same woman from the club the night she
caught him cheating. She remembered that night,
the hurt she had felt as she watched them slow
grind on the dance floor. Deb shook her head in
disgust and turned her back on the ensuing argu-
ment. When she glanced back at them one last
time, she laughed out loud. She had been just in
time to witness the small woman slap Mario smart-
ly across the face.

"See, you sonofabitch, you married to me!" She
stuck her ring finger in his face. "You thought I
was out of town, but I fooled you!"

At that moment Deb finally realized she no
longer loved or even cared about Mario. All the
years of drama, other women, and his lies drifted
into the cold night air. For once, she felt free. Free
of all the anxiety, the reservations she had about
being involved with a man. She exhaled deeply and
began to laugh out loud; her anger disappeared
and all she felt was pity for Mario.

Deb looked up and down the street in hopes of
snaring a cab home. Her laughter turned to near

hysterics when Mario tumbled out of the restaurant and fell onto the sidewalk near her.

With a muttered apology to Deb, his wife
crouched over him and began to kick and scratch
at him. "Think you gonna play me for a fool?" she
yelled between blows. He was balled up on the
sidewalk, his arms covering his head. "Oh, no. I
don't think so!"

"Taxi!" Deb called out, her hand high above her
head. A cab swerved to the curb.

"You've had a good night?" the cab driver asked
as Deb scooted in the back seat.

"The best!" she said, still laughing at the scene
she was leaving behind. She wiped droplets of
tears from her cheeks. As the cab sped away from
the curb, Deb turned all the way around in the
seat. She wanted to see Mario get what he
deserved. She could see that his wife had removed
her shoe.

"That's what he gets," Deb said to the cab driver. "And to think I thought I would regret this. Hell,
I wouldn't have missed it for the world."

The cabby laughed as Deb told him about the
incident at the restaurant. She hadn't laughed this
hard since she was with Darrin. Her smile faded.

The streets of downtown Chicago whizzed by.
The street lights made odd shadows inside the cab.
Deb wondered what Darrin was doing at that
moment. She knew that she had been a real ass,

knowing full well that she wanted to be with him, now and forever. But would he forgive her this time? She had asked for more than she asked from herself. And that wasn't fair to him. He was angry and she didn't blame him. Now the question was how to make it right, how to make it up to him.

An odd feeling swept over her; the hairs on her neck stood on end. She knew what to do, something she had never done before. Words from her mother, Shari, even Darrin, flooded her.

"She's right. Mom was right. Dang, even Darrin was right. I'd be crazy to just let him walk away," Deb said to herself as she looked at the buildings and people streaking by.

The cabby glanced at her through the rear view mirror. She ignored him. She knew that she loved Darrin. She loved no other like him, with all of her heart, body, and soul. The evening with Mario had given her the opportunity to see that. It proved to her that Darrin was exactly what she wanted, needed.

"I need him!" she shouted, startling the driver and making him cause the car to swerve.

"What the hell?" He looked at her again in the rear view mirror.

"Driver, turn around! Please! Now! Turn around!"

The cabby punched the brakes. The tires squealed as he made a wild U-turn in the middle of Michigan Avenue.

Deb gave the cabby Darrin's address. "And step on it," she added.

Chapter Twenty

The lobby was eerily quiet, the lights low, as Deb stepped into the foyer of Darrin's building.

"Good evening. How may I help you?" the doorman asked.

"Hello, Mr. Johnson. Do you remember me? It's me, Deb. Darrin's friend?"

"Ah, yes. How are you?"

"I'm okay. Mr. Johnson. I need to go up and see Darrin. It's really important."

"Well, I'll let him know you're here." Mr. Johnson picked up the phone.

"No! Wait." Deb placed her hand on his. "Please don't let him know I'm here. It's complicated and it would take me all night to explain, but I really need to see him."

"I've got all night," Mr. Johnson chuckled then turned serious. "Now, you know I can't let you up there without announcing you first."

"I know, but trust me on this one. He won't be mad, in the least bit, if you let me up without calling first."

"I can lose my job."

"I guarantee that won't happen. Trust me."

"Why is it so important?"

"Mr. Johnson, let's just say that I may have messed up the opportunity of a lifetime," She didn't like the thought that it may already be too late.

"But that's not telling me anything. You could be a woman scorned. You know what I mean?"

"Mr. Johnson, have you seen any women come in with Darrin lately?" As soon as she asked, she wasn't sure she wanted an answer.

"Why? What's the point to all this?"

"My point is that you probably haven't seen Darrin with anyone. But you quite possibly have seen him looking a little...well, how do I put this? Not quite himself?"

"Now that you mention it, he came in here the other evening and he wasn't the normal upbeat young man I know. He nodded when I spoke and walked right on by, didn't say a thing. Did you have something to do with that?" Mr. Johnson eyed her.

"I hate to admit it, but I'm afraid so. I'm the one that caused it and I want to make it right with him, but I need your help."

"Oh, I don't know."

"Mr. Johnson, on the way here I rehearsed over and over what I would say, how to say it, and all I kept coming up with was that I love him. That's all I know. All I want. I need to tell him that to his face. Please, Mr. Johnson," Deb begged. She stood in front of him, unsure of what she would do if he didn't let her up to see Darrin.

The doorman's face softened and he smiled.
"Dang, you gonna cost me my job! Well, shoot! Go
ahead!" he called after her as she ran to the elevator. "And don't you tell him how you got up there!
Hear me?"

The elevator crept upward. She began to prac-
tice what she would say to Darrin when he opened
the door, if he opened it at all.

"Darrin, I'm sorry. I don't want to live without
you." She shook her head and started over.
"Darrin, I know I'm the last person you want to
see...no, that's not right." A pang of guilt tugged at
her as she thought about how badly she had hurt
him. She wouldn't blame him if he never forgave
her. Still she had to tell him how she felt. She
wanted him to know how much she loved him,
wanted him, needed him. And though she prayed
that he wouldn't, she began to contemplate the fact
that he might reject her.

The elevator doors slid slowly open. She stepped
out, looked down the long hallway. She clasped
her hands together and mouthed a small prayer as
she walked down the dimly lit hall.

She faced Darrin's door, her hand raised to
knock. She pressed her ear to the door and heard
the deep baritone voice of Isaac Hayes singing
"Walk On By." The sound of the synthesizer, slow
and pensive, the song's drum beat, filtered out and
into Deb. Tears streamed down her face as she

rested her head on the door, her heart beating wildly.

She wiped her eyes on her sleeve. It was now or never.

She knocked quickly and stepped back. Hours seemed to pass as she stood there. She began to doubt her actions. She had already turned to walk away when the door opened. She stopped and turned to see Darrin, his eyes blank. She couldn't bear the pain etched across his face. It was her fault.

She wanted to speak, reassure him, but after all her rehearsals in the elevator, she didn't know where to begin.

He stood silent, his head slightly cocked to the right.

Before Deb knew it the words poured out. "I can love you, Darrin. I do love you! You hear me? I love you, and I'm sorry for acting so childish. Everything you said was true, Darrin. Even Shari was right. I can't begin to make up for all the pain I've caused you, but I want you to know that I love you and that I'm not afraid to love you. It was cruel and unfair of me to treat you the way I have. I know you are not Mario, worlds from it. I love you, Darrin Wilson. And...well...that's all I came here to say. Bye."

Deb twirled around and walked toward the elevator.

"Deb, wait," Darrin stepped out of his condo. "At least come inside."

She was afraid to turn and face him.

"Please, Deb? I want to talk to you. There are some things I need to say to you."

She hesitated. She wasn't prepared after all for Darrin to reject her. She wanted him, and she didn't want to hear that he no longer felt the same about her.

"Deb? Will you please come in?" he pleaded.

He held the door open. She stepped inside. "Darrin, look, I didn't mean to interrupt you. It was rude for me to come over here without calling."

"Deb, it's okay. Actually, I was just thinking about you. I really wanted to talk to you, to apologize for blowing up at you in Costa Mesa."

"No, Darrin, I'm sorry. I was acting like a frightened child. And that was unfair to you. I lied, Darrin. I lied to you and to myself. Now, the only thing I can do, hope for, is that you will forgive me, again. Can you forgive me?"

She could see his dark eyes were unsure. But at least she had said what she needed to say to him. And she was prepared for him to tell her he never wanted to see her again.

"Please forgive my manners. Would you care to sit down, a drink or something?"

"No, thank you, Darrin. I just came to tell you that."

"Won't you at least sit down? You've had your say. Now let me have mine."

Deb walked to the couch and sat down. She glanced at the pillows near the window. She remembered the first time they made love...it had started there.

He sat near her.

"Deb, I'm the one who should be sorry. I came on too strong. I didn't give you a chance. I acted like a bull in a china shop, revving head first. I should have considered that you may not feel the same."

"Have you heard a thing I said?"

"Yes, I have, but are you sure? I mean what made you change your mind?"

"Mario."

"Mario? What's he got to do with this?"

"I'll explain later," Deb said with a chuckle. "All that matters now is how we feel and getting past all the pain I've caused you. I was afraid."

"Afraid of what, Deb? Couldn't you see how much I loved you, still love you? You have been etched permanently in my mind. My every waking moment is of you, of the way you feel in my arms, of making love to you."

She bowed her head and stood up to look out of the window. A light snow had begun to fall.

"I was afraid of me," Deb said slowly, her back to Darrin. "I was looking for guarantees and I know that they just don't exist."

Deb could hear Darrin move from the couch. He joined her at the window.

"Deb, I forgive you. Why wouldn't I? You don't love someone today and then tomorrow they mean nothing. But I know there is one thing I can guarantee you."

"What's that, Darrin?"

"That I will always love you."

Deb smiled as Darrin encircled her in his arms and rocked slowly from side to side, his head nuzzled atop hers. She turned around and finally looked, really looked into his eyes. She put her hand on his cheek, pulled his face to hers and kissed him full on the lips. He returned the kiss, then released her and looked at her questioningly. She smiled at him, warm and inviting, and he began to kiss her again, this time longer, more intense. She sighed deeply as her arms wrapped around his waist. When he released her, her body was warm and tingling, reacting to his now all too familiar touch.

"You know, I'm going to hold you to that, Mr. Wilson. I'm going to hold you to that guarantee," she whispered and took him by the hand to lead him into his bedroom.

She began to undress him. When she unbuckled his belt, he stopped her and held her hands in his.

"Deb?"

"Yes, Darrin."

"All I ask..." he started before Deb covered his lips with hers. She didn't want to hear words. She wanted to love him. To show him that she loved him, but most important, she wanted to erase the uncertainty in his eyes. With each kiss, she saw his face soften.

"Darrin, I will never hurt you again." She undressed herself.

She made love to Darrin over and over. Each time, her resolve to love him became stronger and stronger. And for the first time, she allowed herself to love and be loved.

Chapter Twenty-one

The lights from the Christmas tree gave off a colorful glow as Darrin and Deb sat at its base, the tree near the window. Earlier they had gone out onto Oak Street, found a tree and bought some decorations. She had teased Darrin when he and the attendant tied the tree to the roof of his car and the sharp pine needles stuck his fingers.

"Oh, what's wrong? Baby don't like the prickly needles?"

"Does it have to be a live tree?" His face was scrunched up into a make-believe pout.

Yet, for all of his protests, he was truly pleased with the nearly six-foot pine tree and the African Christmas ornaments adorning it. She had finished the decorations with several strings of blinking red lights.

She surveyed her handiwork and smiled at Darrin, waiting for his approval. He smirked, then laughed.

"It's okay."

"Okay? I think it's beautiful!"

"It's okay for a Christmas tree," Darrin replied. She lightly punched him in the arm.

"No, Deb it's really nice. I haven't put up a tree in years."

"Now, you'll have to every year."

She stepped over to the window, looked out into the crisp Chicago night, and pointed to a bright star.

"Darrin, come look."

He stood next to her. They both shut their eyes.

"What did you wish for?" he asked her, his arms around her waist.

"I wished that this day would be the beginning of forever."

"Me too." He placed a kiss on her forehead. "Deb, I love you. I will always love you."

"Let's go to bed," she said, a wicked expression on her face.

"Wait. I have something for you."

She sat in front of the tree and let her eyes follow Darrin as he left the room. He returned carrying a large, plain white box. Handing her the box, he joined her on the floor. She glanced at him and shook the box. He grinned. Finally she opened the package, only to find another smaller box inside. Box after box was opened until she reached a small, gold foil-wrapped case.

"Open it," Darrin said. "Sandra helped me pick it out. I hope you like it."

Her hands trembled as she carefully unwrapped the case and opened it. Speechless, she stared at the huge diamond solitaire set in platinum.

Darrin took her hand in his and gently pulled her close.

"This is forever." He kissed her. "Deb, will you marry me? I know it's soon and we have so much more to learn about each other. But you can think about it, and—"

"I love it, Darrin! Yes, yes I'll marry you!"

He jumped up from the floor, pulling Deb with him, and hugged her tightly. He released her, held her left hand in his, and got down on one knee. He placed the ring on her finger.

"Deborah Wilson. I like the sound of that."

She bent and placed a kiss on his lips. He tugged at her. Laughing, they both tumbled over, Deb on top of him.

Darrin was the first to become quiet. He raked his fingers through her hair and she watched that familiar fire build in his eyes. His arms closed around her.

"Merry Christmas, Deb, my love," he said, his voice husky and a little unsteady.

She brushed her lips across his cheek, his mouth. "The first of many Christmases to come. I love you, Darrin. I will always love you."

Epilogue

That August, Deb and Darrin married. Their wedding, attended only by their families and close friends, began at sunrise on the grounds of the Adler Planetarium next to the lake. Chicago's skyline and Navy Pier were the backdrop and added to the romantic air of the morning.

She was dressed in a tea-length fitted taffeta gown. He wore a simple black tuxedo. Their attendants stood by them. Shari, Deb's maid of honor, smiled as she watched Deb walk slowly toward them. Darrin's best man, Mike, patted him on the back.

"You're simply beautiful," Darrin said when his eyes locked with hers.

In the distance, a small string quartet played softly to the rising sun. As the sun peaked, a warm bright orange, they joined hands and pledged their love and support for one another.

They had written their own vows and exchanged them before the minister had them recite traditional ones.

For Darrin, he wanted her to know how much he loved her, and told her so in his words. When it was Deb's turn, she gazed lovingly at him.

"Darrin Wilson," she said.

"Yes, Deb..."

"All I ask..."

Barbara Keaton is a native of Chicago, where she still lives and works in public relations for the Illinois Department of Children and Family Services. She has always had a love of "storytelling," and started writing when she was old enough to pick up a pencil. She began writing her personal journal when she was ten, but it was the little-known order of black nuns, the Oblate Sisters of Providence, at her grammar school who instilled in Barbara a true passion for writing.

Barbara holds a B.A. degree in Communications from Columbia College and a M.S. degree in Journalism from Roosevelt University. *All I Ask* is her first Indigo love story.

INDIGO: Sensuous Love Stories *Order Form*

Mail to:
Genesis Press, Inc.
315 3rd Avenue North
Columbus, MS 39701

Visit our website at

http://www.genesis-press.com

Name——————————————————

Address—————————————————

City/State/Zip————————————————

1999 INDIGO TITLES

Qty	Title	Author	Price	Total
	Somebody's Someone	Sinclair LeBeau	$8.95	
	Interlude	Donna Hill	$8.95	
	The Price of Love	Beverly Clark	$8.95	
	Unconditional Love	Alicia Wiggins	$8.95	
	Mae's Promise	Melody Walcott	$8.95	
	Whispers in the Night	Dorothy Love	$8.95	
	No Regrets (paperback reprint)	Mildred Riley	$8.95	
	Kiss or Keep	D.Y. Phillips	$8.95	
	Naked Soul (paperback reprint)	Gwynne Forster	$8.95	
	Pride and Joi (paperback Reprint)	Gay G. Gunn	$8.95	
	A Love to Cherish (paperback reprint)	Beverly Clark	$8.95	
	Caught in a Trap	Andree Jackson	$8.95	
	Truly Inseparable (paperback reprint)	Wanda Thomas	$8.95	
	A Lighter Shade of Brown	Vicki Andrews	$8.95	
	Cajun Heat	Charlene Berry	$8.95	

Use this order form
or call:

1-888-INDIGO1

(1-888-463-4461)

TOTAL _____

Shipping & Handling _____
($3.00 first book $1.00 each additional book)

TOTAL Amount Enclosed _____

MS Residents add 7% sales tax

INDIGO *Backlist Titles*

QTY	TITLE	AUTHOR	PRICE	TOTAL
	A Love to Cherish	Beverly Clark	$15.95 HC*	
	Again My Love	Kayla Perrin	$10.95	
	Breeze	Robin Hampton	$10.95	
	Careless Whispers	Rochelle Alers	$8.95	
	Dark Embrace	Crystal Wilson Harris	$8.95	
	Dark Storm Rising	Chinelu Moore	$10.95	
	Entwined Destinies	Elsie B. Washington	$4.99	
	Everlastin' Love	Gay G. Gunn	$10.95	
	Gentle Yearning	Rochelle Alers	$10.95	
	Glory of Love	Sinclair LeBeau	$10.95	
	Indiscretions	Donna Hill	$8.95	
	Love Always	Mildred E. Riley	$10.95	
	Love Unveiled	Gloria Green	$10.95	
	Love's Deception	Charlene A. Berry	$10.95	
	Midnight Peril	Vicki Andrews	$10.95	
	Naked Soul	Gwynne Forster	$15.95 HC*	
	No Regrets	Mildred E. Riley	$15.95 HC*	
	Nowhere to Run	Gay G. Gunn	$10.95	
	Passion	T.T. Henderson	$10.95	
	Pride and Joi	Gay G. Gunn	$15.95 HC*	
	Quiet Storm	Donna Hill	$10.95	
	Reckless Surrender	Rochelle Alers	$6.95	
	Rooms of the Heart	Donna Hill	$8.95	
	Shades of Desire	Monica White	$8.95	
	Truly Inseparable	Mildred Y. Thomas	$15.95 HC*	
	Whispers in the Sand	LaFlorya Gauthier	$10.95	
	Yesterday is Gone	Beverly Clark	$10.95	

* indicates Hard Cover

Total for Books _____
Shipping and Handling _____
($3.00 first book $1.00 each additional book)